W9-APW-083

FALSE FACE

BY THE SAME AUTHOR

Witchery Hill

(*A Margaret K. McElderry Book*)

Margaret K. McElderry Books
NEW YORK

Originally published by Douglas & McIntyre, Vancouver

Margaret K. McElderry Books
Macmillan Publishing Company
866 Third Avenue, New York, NY 10022

Composition by Arcata Graphics/Kingsport
Kingsport, Tennessee
Printed and bound by R. R. Donnelley & Sons
Harrisonburg, Virginia
Designed by Barbara A. Fitzsimmons

First United States Edition 1988

10 9 8 7 6 5 4 3 2 1

Library of Congress Cataloging-in-Publication Data
Katz, Welwyn Wilton.
False face.
Originally published: Vancouver:
Douglas & McIntyre, © 1987.
Summary: Thirteen-year-old Laney, troubled by the animosity between her divorced parents, and fourteen-year-old Tom, determined to preserve his Indian identity, form an uneasy alliance after finding rare Indian false face masks and realizing their terrifying power.
[1. Supernatural—Fiction. 2. Indians of North America—Fiction. 3. Family problems—Fiction]
I. Title.
PZ7.K15746Fal 1988 [Fic] 88–12846
ISBN 0–689–50456–X

This book is dedicated to my daughter,
Meredith Allison Katz,
aged three,
whose sunny-natured cooperation
helped make this book
possible.

I want to acknowledge with gratitude
the financial support
of the Canada Council.

Time now to pry
the secrets from your hearts,
preserve them in glass,
on celluloid strips,
or saturated frames
animated to puppetry,
until your mysteries bleed
blood to water,
until they fade to academic
puzzles and we can turn
to our own for pale answers.

—from *Pale Answers*
by Barbara Novak

FALSE FACE

"DON'T FORGET YOU'VE GOT THAT MATH TEST TO STUDY for, Laney. Oh, and Rosemary won't be back till late, so you'll have to look after the dog for her."

Laney McIntyre looked at her mother, poring over next week's auction list in the *Star*. Mrs. McIntyre's eyes were intent on the paper. Her blond hair swung thickly to one side of her even features.

Look after the dog for Rosemary! Laney thought. As if she ever did anything else!

Reaching for the coffeepot, Alicia McIntyre saw her daughter's outraged expression. She grinned. "Oh, all right," she conceded. "We both know Hambone would have to be halfway to doggy heaven before Rosemary did anything for him." She added cream to her cup, giving Laney that quick, blue glance of hers that took in everything at once. "That jacket's nice on you," she said. "If you didn't slouch so, it'd bring out the color of your eyes."

"You don't like green eyes." It was out before Laney could stop herself. "Last week—that TV show guy—you said so, remember?"

"You're not brooding over that?" her mother said. "Green eyes on a *man* was what we were talking about. You're not a man, are you?"

Laney flushed awkwardly. "No, but—" But Dad was. And Dad had green eyes. And people were always saying how much Laney looked like her father.

"You take things too personally, Laney. Is Rosemary still in bed?"

Laney shook her head. "She's in the bathroom," she said. "She's been in there for almost an hour."

"If this new image of hers lasts much longer," Alicia said, "we're going to have to put in a second bathroom." But her voice wasn't annoyed, only amused. Outside, a bird trilled. Through the open window the smell of autumn wafted in. "Where are you off to?" her mother asked, as Laney headed for the door.

"I thought I'd take Hambone for a walk."

"Would you mind getting some more milk? We're almost out."

"Sure. I mean, I don't mind."

Laney saw her mother's eyes on her, contemplative and assessing, their color as blue and cool as a winter's twilight. It was a disturbing look, not at all maternal. It never failed to make Laney uneasy. She turned away from it now, but too hastily, her sudden movement knocking Hambone's leash off its hook. The chain clattered to the floor, taking a chip of paint off the baseboard. "Sorry," Laney muttered, picking up the chain.

Mrs. McIntyre was holding out some money. Her brows were raised. Not one word about Laney's awkwardness, just those raised brows. Silently, Laney took the bills. "Do read the date on the carton, Laney. And buy it at the end of your walk, okay? I want it fresh this time."

Laney took a deep breath, then wordlessly let it out. Her mother had already gone back to the auction list and didn't appear to notice. Laney shut the screen door behind her with the barest hint of a bang.

In the yard Hambone was waiting for her, cross-eyes beaming. He galloped to her side, taking the leash between his teeth and giving her a slobbery nudge. Laney tickled his ears, the tightness in her shoulders relaxing. "Are we going for a walk?" she teased. The big, yellow dog shook his leash and pranced, grinning at her foolishly.

It was still early. The October wind was crisp as new apples. Laney took deep breaths of it, of the smell of crackly leaves and drying mist and somebody's woodstove coming to life. Across the yard, the two maple trees were bare, their branches black against the vivid blue sky. The grass and sidewalk were heaped with leaves, masses of scarlet that skittered and scudded in the cool wind. Laney could feel it lifting her curls like wings. One of them fell across her eyes, and the sunlight turned it from light brown to an unfamiliar gold.

A squirrel chattered at her from a branch, and over

her head a cardinal took a sudden joyride on the wind. All at once she felt free, as light and alive as the swooping bird. "Let's go a long way today," she said to Hambone.

He woofed his agreement, turning at the corner of the house and trotting across the front yard, heading for Riverside Drive and the undeveloped meadow on its other side. He always knew where Laney wanted to go. Today it would be the bog at the meadow's northern end. Laney smiled, following his lead.

At the front walk Hambone made his usual stop at the chrysanthemums Laney's father had planted four years ago. Since Dad had left, they'd gotten blowsy and nasty-smelling and produced hardly any flowers, but no one had bothered taking them out. The first time Hambone had raised his leg on them, shortly after Ian McIntyre had gone, Mom had grinned and murmured, "So much for your neat rows, Dr. McIntyre!" Now, as always, they endured Hambone's assault and refused to die, and now, as always, Laney looked the other way.

Sunday traffic on Riverside Drive was light, and Laney had to wait only a few seconds to cross the road. The entrance to the meadow was between a new church and an old house. It was a weedy, rutted track marked only by a No Trespassing sign. Behind this uninviting beginning the meadow stretched for acres. It was a piece of genuine wilderness, surprising to find in the middle of a large Canadian city like London. Laney's father called it the city's biggest saving grace.

The meadow was to have become a housing development. But there was a bog on its northern limits, and some scientists had decided the bog was too rare and important to risk. They'd persuaded the developer to stop construction in the meadow, and then they named the bog after him. On the other side of the bog there was a boardwalk, so that people could walk in the bog without hurting it. But on this side there was nothing, only the meadow with its grass-covered mounds, which the bulldozers had left, and at the far north end the tree line showing where green and brown slopes descended into natural bog.

People were always saying that the developer was about to begin construction again. "You couldn't blame him," Laney's mother had said once, when Laney had brought it up. "It is his land, after all."

Laney did blame him. She loved the meadow, thick with wild grain and mullein and the rusty brown of curly dock. Even more she loved the cool, sticky bog, the orange touch-me-nots lining the shady paths, the trees all lacy with lichen. She had built forts in the trees that circled the bog. She had explored the lost paths that wandered the spongy land. She had seen cranes drinking in the lily pond at the end of the boardwalk and hunting ospreys circling it. She didn't want there to be any chance at all of the bog being damaged. And a lot of people, including Laney's science teacher, had said it would be if the housing project went ahead.

She kept Hambone on the leash until they were well into the meadow, then let him go free. As usual, he found something to interest him right away. It was a grasshopper this time. Laney laughed as the dog leaped straight-legged into the air, imitating the insect. When the grasshopper disappeared, Hambone gave a mournful sigh, all the while looking for something else.

"You actor." Laney smiled, shaking her head at him.

It had been her mother who had noticed it first. "That dog's the biggest ham this side of Stratford," she'd said, the very first day. He'd been Rosemary's birthday present and nameless until Rosemary had started opening her other gifts. That was when he'd nudged her leg and howled. Except for the speculative look in his eyes, he would have been the picture of misery. Hambone, Alicia McIntyre had called him, and the name had stuck.

Mom wasn't sentimental. It was something Laney envied. Her mother was a businesswoman, an antique dealer who had studied art and archaeology at the university. She had always known what she wanted to do, and smiled at the students who thought the best thing to do with old things was to study them. Ian McIntyre had been one of those students. She had spent the first years of their marriage trying to change him. It was, Laney sometimes thought, the only thing she had ever failed at.

Rosemary had been two years old when Alicia McIntyre had opened Heritage Lane, her antique store on fashionable Richmond Row. When Laney was born a couple of months later, she had been named after the shop. In Alicia's files there was an old article from the *Free Press* about the dual launching of Laney and her namesake. It had been good publicity, at the time. What Dr. McIntyre had thought about it, Laney didn't know.

Her parents were divorced by the time Laney was ten. In the three years since then she had spent every second Sunday with her father. At first she and Rosemary had gone together, but they always ended up doing what Rosemary wanted, because Laney could never think of anything the others would like to do. So then Dad had suggested that the two girls make separate visits. Now Laney spent her Sundays with him, watching rented movies on TV and going out for hamburgers afterwards. Sometimes people would look at them and smile, seeing their identical sandy hair and green eyes and thin, expressive faces. It made Laney a little uncomfortable, but her father never appeared to notice.

Today Rosemary and Dad were going to Ontario Place in Toronto for a rock concert. Once Laney had asked Rosemary what it was like going someplace like that with Dad. "At least you can't hear his watch ticking." Rosemary had shrugged. That was Rosemary. She could always think of something clever to say.

Hambone's yellow body was almost lost in the tall grass of the meadow. Laney let him explore, making her way to the tree line at the meadow's northern end. Here the open grassland disappeared and wooded slopes descended over increasingly damp earth to the bog at the bottom. A lot of different paths went through these woods. The one Laney chose today was narrow and overgrown, cut off from the sky by a weaving of tree branches. She had found it in the summer while walking with her mother and Rosemary after chasing a cat away from a goldfinch nest. Then the path had been a cool, dark tunnel, blocked by spiky stands of willow and thorn and choked with wild grapevines. Both her mother and Rosemary had refused to enter it, and even Laney hadn't gone far. Now, with the leaves falling, the path was much less gloomy, and Laney decided to explore it more thoroughly.

Hambone saw her heading through the thicket without him. With an outraged bark he bounded past her, crashing through the undergrowth until he met a patch of mud, then skidding into a bush. He let his dignity be briefly hurt, then stiffened, his nose twitching at something off the path. Before Laney could stop him, he was out of sight.

She scrambled after him quickly. There were still parts of the bog she didn't know very well, and there was always the chance that the mud might be deep. "Hambone, get back here!" she called. "Hambone!"

She left the path, gingerly pushing her way past the bush where he'd disappeared. Behind it she spotted the faint traces of another trail, one she'd never seen before. Then she saw Hambone. He was covered with mud, rooting like a pig by the shallows of a small, lime-green pond. He lifted his head, saw her coming, and gave an amiable woof. Something small and dark dropped from his jaws. He picked it up again, then trotted over to her, dropping it like a peace offering at her feet.

Nervously, Laney bent over. But it wasn't anything alive. She picked it up, absently rubbing off the mud on her sleeve. It was a strange object, like a small, long-toothed comb. While she was examining it, Hambone went back to his digging place and brought her something else. When it was cleaned off it looked exactly like a pipe, with a carved stone owl at the place where the stem entered the bowl. The wooden stem was broken off close to the end and was in bad shape, but the bowl itself was perfect. There wasn't a chip in it.

Laney had been to the Museum of Indian Archaeology on a school field trip, and she had seen a lot of things there that were just like this. "You genius, Hambone!" she exclaimed. "This is Indian stuff, the real thing! And to think I've never even found an arrowhead!"

Modestly Hambone bowed his head. When he went back a third time to the edge of the algae-covered pond, Laney followed. He started digging again, spurred on by her interest. Mud flew in every direction.

"Hey, stop!" Laney commanded, pulling at his collar. "If there's anything else there, you might hurt it."

He woofed a hurt denial, then settled back, watching as she took off her jacket, put it on the ground, and placed the pipe and comb carefully down on it. But when she began feeling around in the muck, he lost interest. Sitting up on his haunches, he looked behind them, his muddy nose twitching. He gave a small growl, then went and stood beside Laney.

She didn't notice. In the bog she had felt the outline of something palm-sized and solid. With a tingle of excitement she started to pull it out. It was then that a boy's voice spoke behind her.

"Digging for treasure?" it said, hard and familiar sounding. And then, accusingly, "Hey, this is an Iroquois smoking pipe! Don't you know it's against the law to disturb Indian remains?"

Tom Walsh knew something about the laws regarding Indians. On his father's side he was Mohawk, one of the six tribes that made up the Iroquois Nation. His mother, a white woman who had gone to the

Grand River Reserve to research a government report, had met his father there and stayed. But now Tom's father was dead, hit by a car while he was crossing a road at night. After his death Mrs. Walsh had decided to leave the Reserve and take Tom to London, where she had been born.

"London's not so big you'll get lost," she had encouraged him. "There's a native friendship center there, and an Indian museum. The schools are good, too. Native kids are bused there from the Muncey and Oneida reserves. You'll like it, Tom. It's very green, for a city."

"It won't be green, it'll be white," Tom had said, but to himself, so as not to hurt his mother.

He had been right. The house on Riverside Drive was modern, convenient, and well-built. It didn't even have a fireplace. There were no Indians on the weedless walks and way too many other people. They lived so close to one another they could hear each other's nightmares. But no one seemed to know anyone else. It was a community of strangers, too noisy, too bright, too suspicious. He had been here three months, and it felt like forever.

The only thing that made the place bearable was the wooded bog that lay across the road and down from his house. He spent as much time in it as he could. Sometimes he even skipped school to go there. School was a joke, full of kids who couldn't tell a blue jay from a robin. They were white as they come and snobby about Indians. He got into three fights in the first week. After that they left him alone. He kept to himself, answering questions in class only when no one else knew the answer, studying just hard enough to get the best marks in everything except Canadian history. He ignored history. It was a white subject, anyway.

Tom knew Laney McIntyre from school. Like him, she was in grade nine, though she seemed younger. They took science and physical education together, but they'd never spoken to one another. Laney was good in science and terrible in phys ed. It was the contrast that had made him notice her. She did science experiments with the control and delicacy of a robot arm: not graceful, but interesting to watch. In gym, however, she was just a lot of tangled limbs getting in everyone's way. She knew it, too; her eyes were the kind that showed how she felt.

He had been exploring in the bog when he'd heard the dog barking. He recognized Laney's voice before he saw her, and almost went the other way. But she sounded so excited, he was curious. He got there without her seeing him. The dog was on the alert, but Tom hunched to the ground to show him he wasn't anything dangerous, and the long, yellow tail began to wag. Crouching there, Tom got a good look at what was lying on Laney's jacket. The comb didn't mean much to him, but the pipe drew him like a magnet. He knew what it was. He'd seen plenty of Iroquois smoking pipes on the Reserve.

He picked it up, stroking the bowl possessively. A long time ago an Indian craftsman had labored over this with nothing but stone tools to help him. The craftsman was long gone, and his way of life with him, but still the pipe remained. Tom looked at it, thinking of the people whose stone tools, and whose dominion in this country, were gone forever. His heritage, he thought, still fingering the pipe. Resentment rose in him. What was this white girl doing with it?

"Do you have any idea how old this pipe is?" he accused Laney. "Do you even care?"

Laney had turned only her head at the sound of his voice. Her hands were still buried in the muck, still clutching the small, hard thing she had found. She couldn't take it out, not with Tom Walsh watching. And it was equally impossible just to leave it there. Wouldn't you know it would be Tom, creeping up on her like this? Other people wouldn't have cared even if they had noticed the pipe.

"I wasn't doing anything wrong," she defended herself. "Hambone found the stuff. I was just—"

"Making sure he didn't miss anything," he said, looking pointedly at her buried hands.

She jerked her hands free, keeping the right one clenched around the hidden object. Tom's hands were clenched, too, so he didn't notice. Hambone was looking from one to the other of them, trying to understand. His tail had stopped wagging.

"I can dig in the bog if I want to," Laney said. She got to her feet, then shoved her right hand into the pocket of her pants, shoulders hunched guiltily.

"You can dig in a litterbox, for all I care," Tom said. "But this pipe isn't going to be one of your trophies. It's Indian, not white."

"That doesn't make it yours. Anyway, you're only half-Indian." He stared at her so angrily that she flushed. "Besides, things like this are supposed to go to the archaeologists," she blundered on. "My father's at the university—"

"I'll think about the Indian museum," Tom said, staring her down. "The *Indian* museum, I said. I'm not going to let it rot away in some WASP-y old college lab—or in your underpants drawer, either."

Red with anger, Laney said, "*You'll* think about it. *You're* not going to let it rot. Who do you think you are?" She swept up her jacket with the comb still inside. "You didn't find that pipe. You don't have any right—"

"Tell it to Daddy," Tom said rudely.

He watched her until she was out of sight.

WHY HADN'T SHE GRABBED THE PIPE AWAY FROM HIM? Laney raged. Why had she let him kick her around? And the way he'd talked to her! Did he really think she'd keep an Iroquois pipe in her underpants drawer?

Hambone kept close to her, now and then nosing her with his muddy snout. "Fine watchdog you are," she berated him. "You didn't even bark at him!"

They were out of the bog and halfway across the meadow before she cooled down. At least she still had the comb. And there was the thing in her pocket, too, whatever that was. *She* had found that, not Hambone. As she thought about it, the tingle of excitement rose in her again. Her hands itched to hold it, to finger that strange, rough-smooth ridge she had felt through the muck, those two grapelike knobs, the opening beneath. What was it? The desire to take it out of her pocket and examine it was almost overpowering, but somehow she controlled herself. She'd look at it in her own room, not before. She wasn't taking the chance of someone butting in on this, too.

She left Hambone in the back yard. Through the

storm door Laney could hear her mother on the phone in the living room. "They've just left," Alicia was saying. "Can you imagine Ian at a rock concert? I bet he'll treat it like an anthropological study." Her laugh rang out.

Laney slipped inside, then tiptoed down the hall. She was filthy, but when she got to the bathroom door, she passed it by. The thing she'd found was awfully muddy. Better wait to wash until after she'd looked at it. Anticipation jiggled inside her. Before today, she'd never found anything in her whole life worth collecting.

She shut her bedroom door behind her. Her hands were trembling. Silly. Down in the yard she could hear Hambone barking, loud and urgent. She closed the window, shutting out the sound. She reached into her pocket and rubbed the mud off the object while it was still inside. She let her thumb trace the narrow ridge she had felt before. She poked her index finger into the opening. And then, when she couldn't bear it a moment longer, she lifted the little object out.

And she saw, looking at her out of the palm of her hand, a grimacing face, a face so ugly and sad and terrified and terrifying that she couldn't stop herself from screaming.

Taking the pipe had been a good feeling, but once Laney was gone Tom didn't feel any pride in it. Laney's finding the pipe was one thing. Maybe she hadn't meant to keep it; maybe she would even have handed it over to the museum on her own. But *he* hadn't found it. He had stolen it from her. And what was he going to do with it now? He couldn't put it in his own collection. If he did that, he'd always remember how he'd accused her of wanting to do the very same thing.

But he had a right to it, he thought. He was Indian!

Half an Indian, he corrected himself. Neither one thing nor the other.

He'd have to take it to the museum after all.

Miserably he kicked at the pile of mud the dog had disturbed. Suddenly, desperately, he longed for the Reserve. Why did Mom have to come here? he thought. Why did she have to be white?

"Laney! What's wrong?"

Looking very concerned, Alicia McIntyre pushed Laney's door open. Laney was standing very still, her arms behind her back, her eyes white-rimmed and dark green with shock. "Darling, are you hurt? What's the matter?"

"Nothing," Laney mumbled.

"It can't be nothing. You screamed, and you're as white as snow. Did something scare you?"

Laney could only shake her head. She was furious at herself. Screaming like that, making Mom come in. How could she have been so dumb? And nothing to explain it, just a little wooden face that was only a carving and nothing to be afraid of.

Mrs. McIntyre came farther into the room. In the mirror she suddenly saw Laney's mud-covered arms. Her expression changed. "Good grief! I paid fifty dollars for that jacket. Don't you ever—?" With a visible effort, she broke off, making her voice calm. "You've been in the bog, haven't you? What have you got in your hand?"

"I—it's just something I found. A carving."

"May I see it?"

Laney's hand came forward, jerky and slow, as if she had to command it against its will. Mrs. McIntyre took a tissue and grasped the little wooden face with it. Her blue eyes were narrow, her lips slightly parted. She didn't say a word. She just looked at the carving.

On the antiseptic white tissue the little carved face no longer seemed terrible. It was almost triangular in shape and made of hollowed-out wood, like a mask for a doll. Its eyes were close set and bulged like two grapes under the single ridge of its brow, but the pupils were undrilled and blind. The nose was horn shaped and stuck out a long way. The mouth was like a figure eight on its side. Under a thin layer of drying mud, traces of color were visible. The face was divided vertically in half: the left side, black; the other, red. At the top of the head some mucky hair was tied by a leather thong.

"Is this the reason you screamed?" Mrs. McIntyre said.

Laney didn't answer. Her mother sat down on the bed, turned on the bedside lamp, and held the mask under it. After a long moment, still with her eyes glued to the strange little face, she said absently, "It is a bit gruesome, I suppose." Then, her voice suddenly not absent at all, "Where did you find it?"

"The bog," Laney said, trying not to sound stiff.

"Of course. Where in the bog?"

"You mean, exactly?" Her mother's eyes rose to hers, and Laney flushed. "It was off one of the paths," she mumbled, then cleared her throat. What was wrong with her? Why didn't she want to tell? "You know, the one from last summer? The day we found the goldfinch nest?"

"That tunnelly path you insisted on exploring? Yes, I remember it. This mask was there?"

Laney shook her head, determined, now, to be clear. "Not right there. There's another path. It branches off the first one. Behind a bush—lots of thorns, I don't know the kind. Hambone found it, really."

"So he got away from you again?"

"He hardly ever does it anymore," Laney defended him quickly. "Anyway, it was only as far as a little pond, hardly any distance. He started digging there. That's where this mask was."

"Was anything else with it?"

"This." Laney showed her the comb.

Her mother took it from her, examining it carefully. "Very old," she murmured. "Not in great condition, though. Anything else?"

"A pipe. I—lost it again." Somehow she couldn't tell her mother about Tom.

"You *lost* it?" Alicia McIntyre's eyes were a vivid blue.

Laney managed a jerky nod.

"I see." After a measured look at Laney's face, Mrs. McIntyre asked nothing more. "A pipe, a comb, and a miniature mask," she murmured to herself. "Now I wonder . . ." Abruptly she changed the subject. "How long since you took the mask out of the mud?"

"An hour maybe? Why?"

But her mother didn't answer. She only stared at the little mask. It stared back, its blind eyes round with an ancient horror, its open mouth twisted in despair.

Laney wished her mother wouldn't keep looking at it. "Mom," she asked, trying to draw her attention, "if people find something like this mask, do they have a right to keep it?"

Mrs. McIntyre shrugged. "Who's going to stop you?"

"Well, I mean, it's old, isn't it? Shouldn't it go to—well, shouldn't we tell someone?"

"A museum, you mean?" Her mother's voice was tight.

"Dad always says old things belong—" Laney began.

"I know what he says. Don't you start, please."

For a moment neither of them said anything. Then Mrs. McIntyre tried to smile. "Laney, you mustn't forget that it's your father's *job* to send things to museums. But it's not your job, and it's not mine. The fact is, if you hadn't found these things, they would have stayed in the bog forever. A museum would never have even known they existed. Buried in mud or in someone's private collection—your own, say—what's the difference?"

There was a difference, somehow; Laney knew there was. But she couldn't say so. Mom already thought she was too much like her father.

Mrs. McIntyre seemed to take her silence for agreement. She handed the comb back. "You can keep this, at least," she said. "As an artifact, it isn't worth very much, so you can salve your conscience about some museum wanting it." Her voice was sardonic. "It's made of antler, so it won't disintegrate quickly. I expect it'll be around long after you grow bored with it."

"What about the mask?" Laney didn't look at her mother's face. Instead she stared at her elegant white hand, at the long-nailed thumb and forefinger closed over the tissue so that now only a corner of the little carved face showed beneath.

"The mask's wooden, of course. If it hadn't been buried in bog mud, which tends to preserve things, it would have rotted away centuries ago." Her voice was the clear, competent one she used for business. "But it's not in the bog anymore. Unless it's artificially preserved, in three or four days there won't be anything of it left."

Laney blinked up at her mother, at the bland face with its brilliant blue eyes regarding her so narrowly. She felt disoriented; vaguely sick, even. Nothing of the mask left! But the mask couldn't decay! It was hers—it couldn't!

"Dad could save it," she blurted out. She regretted it at once, but it was too late.

Mrs. McIntyre's lips thinned. "I could, too, darling. I took the same courses your father did."

Why am I so dumb? Laney thought. "I know you could, Mom. I—you're—" She broke off. "What would you do with it, after?"

Mrs. McIntyre didn't answer for quite a while. Then, quite pleasantly, she said, "Do you know anything about this kind of mask, Laney?"

"It's Indian."

"Iroquois Indian, actually. It's a false face mask. Full-sized false faces were worn during Iroquois medicine rituals. The miniature ones went along for the ride. Kind of a personal charm, I guess. That's what this is, a miniature false face."

Her voice got quieter. "They're rare, Laney. Old ones like this are hardly ever found nowadays. Collectors will pay a lot of money for them."

Laney stared at her. "You wouldn't sell it!"

"I might act as your agent."

"But I don't want you to. I want to keep it!" It came bursting out of her without thought. She couldn't have kept it in even if she had known she was going to say it.

Alicia's voice went ironic. "You mean you don't want to give it to a museum?"

"You already said—"

"That's right. I did. And every minute we talk, this mask is being exposed to the air. It needs desalting right away, followed by a bunch of alcohol baths and then several more of xylol, acetone, and then acetone with celluloid." Pause. "You see, darling, I do know what I'm doing."

So she was still angry about that comment about Dad.

Laney gnawed at her lower lip. Over and over again, she thought; why can't I *learn*? Trying and trying and then, in one split second, messing it all up: saying something stupid, wrecking her clothes, forgetting things, getting things wrong. Not thinking, just not thinking—and then Mom looking at her like this, with that cool professional smile that could hide almost anything, and the blue gaze taking account, keeping track of everything, comparing.

She raised her eyes. "I didn't mean—"

Her mother said, "Once the mask is preserved, we can finish talking about it. Until we do, I don't think you should mention your finds to anybody. That's *anybody*, Laney." Laney nodded quickly, knowing whom her mother meant. Alicia nodded, then, too. "Right," she said, "I'll get this thing started, shall I?" She started out, then added casually over her shoulder, "By the way, I suppose you didn't remember to get the milk?"

And without waiting for an answer, she left the room, the little false face tucked into her gently pinching grip.

Laney stared helplessly after her. Yes, Mom was still mad. And now the mask was gone, too. Would she ever let Laney have it back?

Alcohol, xylol, all those chemicals. Laney tried to imagine that horror-stretched little face in an alcohol bath, those sightless eyes dripping alcohol tears. But the alternative was worse, wasn't it?

She rubbed her forehead, leaving a muddy streak on her pale skin. There was an icy feeling in the pit of her stomach. What was she afraid of? She had taken an old mask from a bog; that was all. Why was she so sure that now nothing was going to be the same?

Tom was down on his knees, scrabbling with both hands in the mud. He didn't know why he hadn't thought of it before. An Indian pipe had been found here. Why not something else? Laney had obviously thought so. She'd been searching when he'd arrived.

He felt something almost at once, a hard, solid object

too big to be a stone. It was wrist-deep in mud and firmly wedged. He explored it with his fingers, but couldn't find anything to pull on. It felt like wood, though, probably carved. What was it? His excitement grew. Under the excitement there was another feeling, something darker, but he wouldn't let himself recognize it. He tried to imagine what he had found. Something big, he thought feverishly, handmade, carved. Whatever it was, it must be even more important than the pipe. Maybe he ought to call an archaeologist. But no. It was his find.

If he made himself be careful, he told himself firmly, he wouldn't damage it.

He ploughed aside the top layer of mud, then slowly, a thimble's-worth at a time, began removing the rest of the layers. It took a long time. The October sun climbed higher. In this part of the bog it brought no warmth, only the deeper shadow of the hill behind. The wet rose like a squeezed sponge into his jeans. Tom didn't notice. He was an archaeologist, doing his first dig. He didn't even know he was afraid.

And when he finally found out, it was too late.

There was a dead man in the bog.

He wore a mask.

It was the face of a god.

Gaguwara! Tom addressed it, fending it off. *Gaguwara!*

The blind eyes leered, freed from the weight of

centuries, a dark god's likeness caught in that skin of wood.

Danger. Danger. Impossible to bury it again. Impossible not to. Tom ran, breath sobbing, feet thudding. He was all Indian now, an Iroquois fleeing for his life.

Behind him, the black and red divided mask was motionless. Its horn-shaped nose was clogged with mud, and its wooden lips wore a grimace of perpetual pain. No one owned it now, not even the dead man.

The boy had refused to claim it.

DINNER WAS OVER. ROSEMARY WAS STILL AT THE ROCK concert. Mrs. McIntyre had excused herself right after the meal, saying she had work to do. Laney was left alone in the kitchen, trying to get her homework done so that she could study for her math test on Tuesday. But it was hard to concentrate. Her mother's face, and the mask's, kept on getting mixed up in her mind.

Four-sevenths minus seven-eighths. Now did you get a common denominator, or did you cancel? With fractions, it might be either.

Mom had seemed tired at dinner. What had she been doing all afternoon? Not just looking after the little mask; that was for sure. About an hour after she'd taken it down to her workroom, Laney had caught a brief glimpse of her leaving the house, tramping off in Dad's old rubber boots down the drive. She'd been gone for hours. Then, about midafternoon, when Laney was trying to coax Hambone into the tin tub that served as his bath, she'd heard the car start up in the drive, and seen her mother's profile above the steering wheel.

And not a word to her, Laney thought now. Not even good-bye.

Canceling was easier than finding a common denominator. But Mr. Hardwick never gave easy homework. Okay, so canceling was no good. A common denominator, then. Something seven and eight both went into. Seven and eight. Seventy-eight?

She wrote it down. It looked all right. At least it made more sense than seeing Mom, of all people, wearing rubber boots.

It was very quiet in the house. Mom was probably down the hall in her workroom, but she wasn't making any noise. The little mask would be there, too.

Maybe Mom would like some tea, Laney thought suddenly. She shoved her book aside and reached for the kettle. Fractions were out of date, anyway. Computers were what counted now, and everybody knew computers worked only in decimals.

Tom Walsh was in his room. His homework for Monday waited on his desk, but he ignored it, polishing the Iroquois pipe instead. What was left of the wooden stem was warping quickly, and there was a split in the wood that hadn't been there before. But under his touch the stone bowl of the pipe was coming to life, gleaming and warm. The little owl was looking so real he almost expected its eyes to blink.

Through his open door Tom could hear his mother

splashing in the bathroom. Since they'd moved in here she took a bath every morning and every night. Twice a day, going in clean, coming out clean. Tom couldn't understand it.

On the Reserve she'd seemed like everybody else.

He hadn't told her about *Gaguwara*. He hadn't told anybody. Ever since finding it this morning, he'd been trying to believe he'd imagined it. Or, at least, that he'd imagined the feeling it had given him.

It was an old mask; that was all. How could it be more than that?

But he heard a soft echo from the longhouse,

> *It might happen, It might happen*
> *ha i ge ha i*
> *They stir us, the great False Faces,*
> *sayokiya donyano sagodyo wegowe so'o.*

The Indian pipe was glowing, warm with friction. But pale, he thought, empty of fire. The bathroom was silent. He might have been alone in the world. In a longhouse, somewhere, a box turtle was rattling the spirits away.

Mrs. McIntyre wasn't in her workroom. For a short moment Laney stood in the doorway, the tea tray in her hands. Across the room she could see her old goldfish bowl, now full of alcohol. The mask was in it, half-floating, its empty eyes facing the other way.

Laney put down the tray. Then, slowly, she went

toward the mask. The floor was carpeted, supported by a steel beam that ran the length of the house. Laney was small and light, her footsteps virtually soundless. But somehow at her approach currents formed in the still fluid, and the drifting mask swiveled to face her.

Laney looked at it. I shouldn't have taken it, she thought. I should never have started this.

But it was too late.

She turned her back on it and went away. The blind eyes followed her out the door.

Tom was late for school the next day, missing half his art class, his favorite. He'd been phoning the Indian museum about the Iroquois pipe. They were pleasant enough to him, but cautious. Probably thinking he was just a kid who didn't know anything about old things, he thought. Well, they'd find out tomorrow, when he showed the pipe to them.

He saw Laney at school after first period, but she was being yelled at by Mr. Hardwick and didn't see Tom. In science she bumped into him at the door. "Sorry," she said automatically, then stiffened, seeing who he was.

"My fault," Tom started to say, but Morry Robbins shoved between them, and he didn't know whether to be glad or not.

The last class of the day was gym. The girls saw a

movie while the boys did calisthenics, and then, nudging and giggling, they changed over. Tom had never seen the movie, but he knew it all anyway. He saw Laney coming out of the gym afterwards. She was walking slowly, staring down at the floor. He didn't intend to speak to her. It was as much a surprise to him as it was to her when he did.

"I called the museum today," he said.

"The museum?" She blinked at him.

"About the pipe." He didn't know why he wanted to tell her.

"Oh. That." Pause. "What did they say?"

"I'm taking it over tomorrow, after school." Another long pause. "I'll tell them it was you who found it," he offered.

"No, don't."

A thought hit Tom, making him blink. There was no way he could tell the museum people about Laney. Because they would want to know where the pipe had been found, and Laney would have no reason not to tell them. As soon as she did, they would troop out there, all those Ph.D.'s and curators and excavators and you-name-its, thinking they just might find something else in the same spot. And they would, too. They would find the body, and they would find the twisted *face* it wore.

They would take it out of the muck and put it on display.

"All right, I won't tell them," he promised.

"Laney! Hey, Laney!"

It was Laney's older sister, Rosemary. Tom had seen her now and then, a semipunker whose good looks never ran second to the style. Grade eleven and owned the halls. She was with Webster Irving, a bubblehead with big biceps. "Take my binder home with you, huh, Laney?" she called across the crowded hall. She was eyeing Tom curiously. "Web and I are going to get a Coke."

She wasn't the only one to be looking at Tom and Laney. Everyone in the whole school seemed to be doing the same thing.

"I have to go," Laney said.

Tom raised his head proudly. His cheekbones were sharp as axe heads. "See you," he said, and swaggered away.

When he was back on the third floor again, he allowed himself to hurry. He threw his books into his locker, then grabbed his jacket and headed for the nearest variety store. "I want some cigarettes," he said to the man behind the counter.

"Brand?"

Tom didn't smoke. "Those," he said, pointing. The man looked at him more closely, and Tom's chin rose. "Getting them for my mother," he lied.

"That's what they all say," said the man, handing him the package.

Defiantly, Tom added, "I'll have some creamed corn, too." It wasn't exactly corn mush, but he hoped it would do. But what about the bear fat?, he thought, out on the street again. He went back into the store and bought a pound of lard.

A whole day, now, since he'd seen *Gaguwara*. He shouldn't have left it so long.

He hurried home. Mom was still at work. Quickly he took the tobacco out of the cigarettes, then borrowed his mother's dutch oven and a can opener. Then he went to the bog.

"That's right, Indian masks," Laney said to the librarian. "Maybe they'd be called false faces." That was what Mom had called them, hadn't she?

"Is it a school project?" the librarian asked, whiffling competently through the microfiches.

Laney tugged at her hair. "No."

"We don't have an entire book on them," the woman said after a minute. "There might be something on them in one of these, though." She wrote down some titles and call numbers. "Do you have an adult card?"

"Er—"

"Because if not, you can't take the books home, you know."

"That's all right," Laney muttered. She wouldn't have taken them home anyway.

She followed the librarian's directions, then began

pulling out books. She sat down at one of the tables and turned to the index of the first book. Nothing. She tried another. In the fifth book, she found it. *False Faces:* see *Society of Faces, False Face God, False Face Sickness, Miniature Masks.* Nervously, she began reading.

A red-faced old man with unmatching socks sat down at the table, opened the Business Monday section of the *Free Press,* and immediately began snoring. In the stacks behind her a couple of elementary school girls giggled over an anatomy textbook. A clerk chose a spot right beside Laney to unload his cart piled with returned books. Laney didn't see any of it.

It was a long time before she finished reading. In a daze she got up from the table. Her chair leg caught on the old man's foot. He opened one eye, snorted at her, and went back to sleep. She didn't notice. When she came out of the library, a blast of cold wind hit her in the face. She looked across the lines of traffic to the renovated old buildings, people hurrying home to them from work. She listened to car engines humming and church bells chiming the hour. She smelled fallen leaves and cooking hot dogs and gasoline fumes. London, she thought, comforted. Home.

But long ago, Indians had occupied this country and built longhouses and worshiped spirits. Here the Society of Faces had gathered with their rattles and their staves and their masks and had gone from longhouse to longhouse, curing disease, or causing it, their power random and dual and terrible. The power of the masks, Laney thought. The masks that made their owners a kind of false face god themselves.

Except that they weren't gods; they were only humans. And power like that was more than any human should handle. To protect themselves from the full-sized masks they wore in their ceremonies, they would make little masks in the likeness of the large and tie them with leather thongs to the larger masks. But these miniature masks, too, were magic. They, too, could harm as well as protect. They, too, carried the danger of the false face god.

And that's what I found, Laney thought.

If it was the real thing.

If it wasn't all just a bunch of superstition, anyway.

The street lights came on. Laney looked at her watch and yelped. Even if she made the next bus, she wouldn't be home until past six-thirty. Mom would have a fit.

The normalcy of the thought was almost comforting.

"You *what?* Mom! Laney went and lost my binder! All my notes are in it! And I've got homework to hand in to Renfrew tomorrow. *Mom!*"

"I didn't lose it," Laney protested, through the calliope of Rosemary's voice. "It's at the library. I remember exactly where I put it. It's on the table with—" With all those books, she finished silently.

"The library will be closed," Mrs. McIntyre said,

"so that doesn't help Rosemary very much, does it? It really is too bad of you, Laney."

"Renfrew'll kill me!" wailed Rosemary.

"I'll write you a note for Mr. Renfrew, Rosemary." She turned to Laney. Her voice was too quiet. "After all those years living with your father, you ought to know how I feel about this sort of business. Late for dinner, forgetting things all the time—"

"I'll get her binder back. I'll go back there tomorrow, as soon as the library opens."

"Thus creating a convenient excuse to miss your math test."

"I wasn't. I—"

"Rosemary will pick up her binder herself. No one can trust you to do what you say."

"I just forgot it! Once, that's all!" Laney was unable to keep her mouth from trembling. "She shouldn't have asked me to take it, if it was so darned important. She should've—"

Her mother snorted. "Should, shouldn't, what difference does it make? You took Rosemary's binder, and you were careless with it. That's what matters, nothing else."

But it wasn't the stupid binder that mattered to Mom; it was Rosemary. Rosemary was always what mattered. "You're always on her side!" Laney burst out wretchedly. "You always—"

Mrs. McIntyre slammed her hand on the table. "Not

the green-eyed monster routine again! Listen to me, Laney! I have always treated you two girls exactly alike. When Rosemary gets a new outfit, you get a new outfit. When Rosemary gets a raise in her allowance, so do you. I even balance how much money I spend on each of you at Christmas, for God's sake! If Rosemary had lost *your* binder, I'd have been just as angry with her as I am with you. Do you hear me?" She clamped her mouth shut, lips thin and twisted with impatience.

"I'm sorry," Laney whispered. Her voice was trembling now, as well as her mouth. "The binder—what you said—I'm really sorry."

After a moment, her mother sighed. "You're always sorry, Laney. I'll give you that at least; your father never was." She reached out to brush Laney's hair away from her eyes. Then she pushed back her chair. "All right, there's nothing we can do about it now. So let's just forget it, okay?"

"But—"

"You've got a math test tomorrow. Hadn't you better get to work?"

And as Laney turned blindly away, Rosemary said, "It's just arithmetic, Mom. They don't even start the hard stuff till Christmas."

Tom went right to his room after supper on Monday. He lay on his bed, staring up at his ceiling, where the moon shadows danced. The street noises were muffled tonight, shut out by the window he had closed, the radio he had turned on loud. He wished he could as easily shut out his memories of the bog.

All that stuff he'd taken with him this afternoon: the tobacco, the corn mush, the lard . . . And the way he'd made himself tall, pushing through the bushes with his kettle, letting branches slap his face rather than bowing, in case *Gaguwara* should discover his fear. He had known exactly what he was going to do. It was what the Society of Faces always did with a mask that needed propitiating. He was going to burn some tobacco and anoint the mask with corn mush. He was going to say some prayers. And then he was going to bury the mask again, returning it to the earth, where it belonged.

But when he arrived there, it had been all for nothing. The mask was gone. The face it had covered lay exposed, a shape of mingled flesh and bone. Rotting before his eyes.

There was a knock on his door, and his mother entered. "Tom? I heard your radio. You're not asleep, are you?"

"No," he said, turning on his bedside lamp.

"You were very quiet at dinner," Jill Walsh said, polishing her glasses on her skirt, the way she always did when she was uncomfortable. "Do you feel all right?"

Silence. He wanted to tell her. But she wouldn't

understand. All that time on the Reserve, and still she wouldn't understand. "I'm fine," he said at last.

"Well, that's good." She tried to smile, putting her glasses back on. She didn't quite look at him. So she didn't believe him, Tom thought.

"It's—something Indian," he got out then, trying to explain, to make her feel better.

Her chin went up. "I lived on the Reserve for a long time," she replied. "I know a little about what it's like to be Indian." She waited, but he didn't speak. Twisting a strand of sandy-colored hair around her ring finger, she added hesitantly, "I also know what it's like to be the only one around with the wrong skin color. Is that what's bothering you? Do you feel left out in London?"

He only looked at her.

"I'm still the wrong color," she said sadly, "aren't I?"

When she was gone, Tom got out of bed. How could I have told her?, he thought, pacing back and forth, back and forth, his shadow a crooked giant on the white, antiseptic walls. On the Reserve, at the False Face ceremonies, had she danced the Round Dance? Had she ever summoned the Society when one of the family got sick? Would she have let them blow ashes in her face?

Every Sunday on the Reserve, Mom had gone to the Methodist service at Stoneridge. The old stone church was only a mile or so away from Onondaga Longhouse, but the two might have been a world apart. When Tom was old enough to choose, he stopped going to church with her. His father didn't care, but still Tom went to the Longhouse. He learned the code of the Iroquois prophet, Handsome Lake; he decided which side of the clan he would join; secretly he practiced the men's dances and sang the rituals. Even his father never knew.

Each day after Mr. Walsh came home from his job at the canning factory, he would listen while Tom talked—hardly speaking himself, but listening so carefully it was easy to tell him things; then he'd read what his wife had written on her novel that day; and then, finally, at supper, they'd all talk. It was never nitpicking stuff about jobs or people or things they wanted to buy. Maybe somebody'd say something about a bird that had suddenly shown up after a winter's absence, and then somebody else would ask how the bird knew when to migrate, and that would lead to the daylight cycle and the movements of the sun. They were never very long conversations, an hour at most. Then George Walsh would head off for a long evening of making stone carvings to sell to the tourists at Min's. Tom missed those supper conversations. He missed them more than anything else about his father. After his father had died, supper had become a time of silence.

George Walsh had never gone in for drinking, the

way some Indians did. That made it even harder to take, that a drunken driver had killed him. He was buried on the Reserve, in the tiny cemetery Tom had just been able to see from the rotting back porch of their house on the Fifth Line.

From the house on Riverside Drive, Tom looked out the window at the drifting moon. Was it really the same moon that shone down on the Reserve? They seemed so far apart, this city and the Reserve. Yet here he was, a link binding the two. And here, too, was *Gaguwara*, the face of an Iroquois god.

Here, or somewhere.

Gaguwara, he thought now, looking out at the moon. Where are you, *Gaguwara*?

Did Laney have the mask? Had she come back to the bog yesterday after he had run away, and had she found the mask there, open to view?

Or was it someone else?

Whoever had taken it, it had been Tom who had exposed *Gaguwara*, Tom who had freed the mask from its prison. If something bad came of it, it would be Tom who would be responsible.

And the moon drifted, and the shadows tossed, and the headlights on Riverside Drive came less and less frequently, and still Tom stood at his window and did not think of sleep.

HE HAD BEEN TALL, AS A YOUNG MAN. WHEN HE FIRST went into the forest to carve the mask, he had been the strongest man in the village. But something had happened that day in the forest. Maybe he had burned too little tobacco as he prayed to the tree and to the *faces*. Maybe his stone knife had cut too deep into the living basswood. Or maybe, as the Faith Keepers said, the spirits were angry at Mankind that day. He came out of the forest with a blind mask and a crooked body, and from that day forward his magic was terrifying.

He had had no wife and no children. He had nothing to outlive him but his pipe and his mask. No one knew where he lived. The only times he was ever seen, except in the ceremonies, were when he went walking in the bog. But when the spirits called, he came. He had been, in turn, Runner, Dancer, and Doorkeeper. In more than one ceremony he had been the Great Doctor himself. And it was on one of those occasions, wearing his blind mask during the Round Dance, that he died.

Afterward, someone found the miniature mask on the longhouse floor, where he had lost it. Its protection had failed him, and so he had died. They were afraid of his bones and would not give them to the ossuary pit. They were even more afraid of the mask. And so they buried him in the bog, because it was far enough away and because he had chosen it in his life. They buried the mask, too, not daring even to take it off his face. With the courtesy of brothers they left him his pipe and some tobacco, food and weapons for the afterlife, a comb for his hair, a beaded belt for ornament. The miniature mask they dropped on the mud they had heaped on him. And then they went away.

There was good hunting in the bog, but no one from the village ever went back.

Laney got up late the morning of her math test. She hadn't fallen asleep until long past midnight. Her sleep had been exhausting as a marathon, nightmare strewn and terrifying. Once, just as the moon was setting, she had sat bolt upright in bed, panting with suffocation and prying at her face as if to tear something off. It had taken a whole glass of water and a walk around the room with the overhead light on to make the horrors go away.

She read her math text while she waited for Rosemary to get out of the bathroom. After three pages she realized she didn't remember a word. She gave up then. She knew she was going to fail.

The bathroom door opened at last. "You're going to be late again," Rosemary said, standing in the way. She had on a new kind of eyeshadow and looked at least twenty.

Laney shoved by her. "If you didn't take so long, I'd be halfway to school by now. Anyway, you usually wake me up."

"Mom said it's time you started taking responsibility for your own actions."

"So get me an alarm clock that works," Laney snapped. "Or how about a clock radio with a decent station on it? I'm sick and tired of your stupid rock all day and all night."

"Wheeew," Rosemary said, "will you listen to her?" And as Laney slammed the door behind her, Rosemary added nastily, "Better not open your eyes too wide today. You might bleed to death."

Laney scowled into the mirror. Green eyes bloodshot and shadowed, colorless face creased with tiredness, curls that stood up in all the wrong directions like independent brown haystacks. . . . She did look terrible, Rosemary was right about that. Rosemary, of course, was right about everything. Laney splashed cold water into her face, knowing it wouldn't help. Viciously she brushed her teeth. Of course I'll give you a note for your teacher, Rosemary, darling. A new radio? Of course, Rosemary, darling. You want to be out late? Whatever you say, Rosemary, darling. And,

Laney, you just better start taking responsibility for your own actions!

She dragged a comb through her hair, then defiantly brushed on a lot of Rosemary's blusher. It made her look like a clown. Rosemary never did, no matter how much she put on. Well, so what? So what if Rosemary looked good and understood math and always knew what to say? So what if it was Laney who had to try, and Rosemary who didn't? So what, so what, so what?

She stomped down to the kitchen. There was no one there. The table was littered with cornflakes and dirty cups and bowls. It was Tuesday, Mom's Toronto day. Mom wouldn't be home till past seven, and she'd be expecting the house to be clean and the casserole in the oven. Rosemary wouldn't care. She'd come home when she felt like it, and she sure wouldn't raise a finger in the kitchen.

Which leaves me, Laney thought. Well, I won't. To hell with her. To hell with them both. I just won't.

Outside, Hambone scratched at the door. Rosemary hadn't even bothered to let him in. His water dish was empty, too. Laney filled it, patting his neck while he drank. He nuzzled her, then cocked his head to one side, as if puzzled by her Peach Puff cheeks. "Okay, okay," she told him and rubbed them clean with the dishcloth. While she had the cloth in her hand, she wiped off the table, too. When that was done, she washed the dishes. And then she swept the floor.

It was quarter to nine when she finished. She gathered up her books and went to the garage to get her bicycle. It had been a couple of weeks since she'd used it, and she'd forgotten that the tires were low. Now she looked at them and groaned. Both flat. No way to pump them up in time. Seven blocks to school, and only ten minutes to do it in. She began to run. And math was first period, too. It was going to be an awful day.

Art class was to be held out of doors today. Art, especially painting, was something Tom liked. Not watercolors, they were too wishy-washy for him. But oil, that he loved, thick and strong, spreadable as butter. He never bothered with outlines or preliminary sketches. He dabbed on color, bits here, great splashes there; and somehow his trees always looked more alive than anyone else's, his rivers more like real water.

He was last out of the art room, trailing the others down the hall, when he saw Laney coming out Mr. Hardwick's door. She was very white, her eyes red rimmed, as if she hadn't slept very well or had been crying. When she shut the door behind her, it was a little too hard, almost a slam. Through the glass in the door Tom could see her classmates bent over their desks, taking a test. "Hardwick kick you out?" he asked.

"I was five minutes late," she said, her chin high. "I don't care. I hate math."

"Everybody hates math when Hardwick teaches it." Mr. Hardwick taught most of the grade nine math classes. "Read pages thirty-five and thirty-six," Tom mimicked, "and do questions one to one thousand on page thirty-seven." He was a lousy teacher.

"You do okay, I bet."

He shrugged. "Last year's stuff, sure. The Reserve has teachers who know how to teach." Over his shoulder, he saw that all the rest of his class had disappeared.

"You'd better go," Laney told him, "before you get kicked out, too."

"You supposed to go to the office or what?"

"I'm supposed to," she said.

"What's that mean?"

"I'm not going. I'm getting out of here." She turned her back on him and began to fiddle with the padlock on her locker. "Everything I do is wrong anyway," she said, her voice muffled.

Ask her about *Gaguwara,* he told himself. But his art teacher had come back to the outside door and was looking in at him. This was no time to play lawyer.

"If you are going to skip, make sure you don't go out the front door," he warned her. Then he left. He would have bet almost anything that Laney McIntyre had never skipped school a day in her life.

She took a bus downtown. At loose ends, she wandered through some stores. In Birks she saw a brass

Chinese checkers set. That made her think of Susan Fine, her best friend since nursery school, now moved away to Ottawa. Two summers ago they had spent a whole month of rainy days playing Chinese checkers. This past summer they'd tried playing again, but Susan was leaving in July, and the game had seemed a waste of time.

Laney winced at the price tag on the set. All around her were mothers and clerks and grandmothers, and they all seemed to be looking at her. Wondering why she wasn't in school, probably. She got on another bus then, not caring where it was going. It was only ten-thirty. She had no idea how she was going to fill in the day. She made her way down the aisle, looking for an empty seat.

"Laney," a quiet voice said.

Her whole body jerked. It was her father, pointing to the seat beside him. "Dad! What're you doing here?"

His green eyes regarded her calmly. "Going to work," he said, waving a hand at the "University" sign on the front windshield. "Parking on campus this late in the day is impossible. I'm afraid I overslept."

"Me, too." It was out before she had a chance to think about it.

"That why you're not in school?"

She looked into her lap. What was the point of lying? He'd find out sooner or later. Everybody would. "I was late for my math test," she said, cold and hard. "Mr. Hardwick wouldn't let me take it."

He was silent for a while. When he did speak, his voice was mild. "Would you have passed it?"

"No."

Another long silence. "I was bad at math for years," he said at last.

"You were? When did you stop being bad?"

"When people gave up pushing me about it. I'd never been good at math to start with, and early on I decided that if I was going to be no good, well then, I'd be no good and proud of it. Not the best attitude, I suppose."

"I wish I could be like that," Laney said, her voice low. "Proud of it, I mean. But I just keep trying and trying. Dumb, eh?"

He eyed her thoughtfully. "Trying's fine, as long as you're doing it for the right reasons," he said. "To please yourself, I mean; not—"

He broke off. "Anyway, eventually I discovered the slide rule. The caveman's calculator," he added, as she looked questioningly at him. "Without that slide rule, I'd have gone through life convinced I couldn't do math. And the funny thing was, I really could do it."

"You could?"

"I got stubborn about trying, early on. But that slide rule was something new, not real math, just a gadget. I didn't have to be stubborn about it. I figured out on my own how to use it, and then, once the slide rule started getting me some right answers, I began to wonder how something I controlled could do it if I couldn't.

So then I tried the math on my own. It seemed a lot easier when I knew I could always get the right answer the other way." He grinned, his face going very young.

The stores of Richmond Row slid by. Across the street, they passed the showroom window of Mrs. McIntyre's store. Neither of them looked at it. A few blocks later, Laney asked wistfully, "Can you do fractions with a slide rule?"

"No, more's the pity."

"Not with a calculator, either, I bet."

Suddenly Dr. McIntyre reached up and pulled the bell. They were at Oxford and Richmond now, only halfway to the university. "Come on," he told a startled Laney.

"Where are we going?"

"We're going," Dr. McIntyre said firmly, "to buy you a calculator, a brand-new, whiz-kid calculator. It's just come out. And guess what? It does fractions!"

Waiting for her mother to come home that night, the casserole in the oven, the kitchen tidy, Laney thought over what had happened. A whole day with Dad. A *good* day. They had bought the calculator, and then they'd had lunch in a Chinese restaurant, and then they'd gone to a hardware store and bought two alarm clocks, one for each of them. After that Dr. McIntyre took her to the university and showed her where he worked, and they spent a couple of hours with the calculator. It was a complicated instrument, but fun, too, and for the most part Laney figured out how to use it on her own. She practiced while her father taught a class, and then they went for a Coke before he took her to the bus and said good-bye. There hadn't been much joking around, nothing like the give-and-take Mom and Rosemary were so good at, but Laney felt as happy as if there had been. Not once in the entire day had she listened for her father's watch to tick.

He gave her something else besides the calculator and the clock. It was a note for the principal of Laney's school. On the bus going home, she read it half a dozen times.

To the principal of Riverview Secondary School, it said. *Laney McIntyre was out of school on Tuesday, October 17, with my permission. She will make up any schoolwork she has missed.*

Signed, Ian McIntyre, her father.

She still couldn't believe it.

It was quiet in the house. Rosemary was across the street at her friend Joanne's. Laney got out her math text and her calculator and did her homework from the night before. Question after question, and always the right answer, always dead easy. It was almost fun. Maybe Dad was right. Maybe making the right answers come up, however you did it, showed that math wasn't impossible after all.

Six-thirty. Half an hour till Mom's train from Toronto came in.

Restlessly, Laney got to her feet. She didn't know where she was going until she got to the workroom door.

The room was shadowy, but she didn't turn on the light. The miniature mask was floating on its back, face to the ceiling. Slowly, Laney approached it. For a long time she looked at it. Wisps of thoughts came into her mind, dreamlike, drifting. Smoke, campfire blue and flickering; muddy moccasin prints on bare stone; a deer with its head cocked; ashes flying about. Voices singing, *Hahehe he we-heyo dewe-ho dewa-ha hu hoi.* The soft sigh of grass underfoot, the rattling of cherry pits in a shell, the beat-beat-beat of drums . . .

"What *are* you doing, standing here in the dark? Laney!"

The light flashed on. It was seven-thirty. Her mother was home.

"BUDGETS!" TOM'S MOTHER SIGHED. SHE TOOK OFF HER glasses, rubbed her forehead, and pushed the big, blue ledger away.

Tom looked up from his book. "What's up?"

"We eat too much," his mother said wryly.

"Are we broke?"

"No, it's not that bad. It's just that now and then I'd like to be able to put something aside for emergencies. But somehow my salary just doesn't stretch that far. And what I get for my stories doesn't keep us in postage stamps."

Tom reached for the ledger. "Wow! Is that what we pay for rent? Couldn't we get something cheaper?"

"Not in a house. And not this near the river or your beloved bog."

He frowned. "You didn't get this white-walled little box because of me, did you?"

"Walls can be painted," Mrs. Walsh said, avoiding his question. "You were going to when we moved in, remember?"

Yes, Tom thought, but that was before he'd known what things were like here. What was the use pretending this place could ever be home? "On the Reserve we didn't need to paint to know we were home," he said. "On the Reserve—"

"On the Reserve we didn't even have a decent bathroom," his mother said sharply.

"We had lots of other things, better things!" His hands were clenched. "We should have stayed there. It's where we belong."

"*I* didn't belong there," his mother said. "I never belonged. I was just George Walsh's white wife. And when he died, I wasn't anything at all."

She turned away. Tom was horribly afraid she was going to cry. She went on at last. "Anyway, how could we have stayed? Your father didn't have much life insurance. I didn't have a job, only my writing. How did you expect us to live?"

Her voice echoed. Tom couldn't think what to say. He still had the ledger. His eyes went over and over the page. "You forgot the telephone bill," he mumbled finally.

"Why don't you help me, Tom?" she asked, sadly and wearily.

He pretended she meant the budget. "What do you think I'm doing?" Blindly he stabbed at the page. "You forgot your car insurance, too."

She knew him too well to push it. They bent over the ledger together then, making lists, reminding each other of expenses that were coming up, adding, subtracting, planning, pretending. And when it was all over, and they had a budget they were pretty sure they could live with, his mother said, "You're like my father, Tom. You've got his knack for organizing."

He knew what she was up to. She was reminding him he wasn't all Indian. Reminding him that maybe there were things in him that were white. He pushed back his chair and went to his room.

Not that there wasn't some truth in what she'd said, he told himself later. He did like organizing things. He liked seeing things labeled and sorted out. Today at the museum, while waiting for the curator to be free, he had taken the pipe into the display area. He liked seeing the centuries spread out before him. He liked the feeling of history it gave him, the awareness that everything was connected. Things made sense, he thought. Everything had a place. Everything belonged somewhere.

And he had been proud, too, proud of his heritage. Waiting for the curator to come, he had wandered the cool, windowless rooms with their scientifically lit cases. Birdstones, pottery, hand-carved awls, pipes, beadwork . . . It was a culture, and it was beautiful. It was his own.

And then he had overheard a visitor say quietly to his companion, "They call it the Indian Museum, but this is the first time I've ever seen one come."

He's talking about me, Tom had thought.

"Preserving old things isn't something most Indians care about," the other man said. "Songs, yes, and language—that sort of thing means something to them. But not this stuff. To them it's buried garbage."

Was it true?

Tom had looked down at the pipe he had polished so lovingly. Garbage? He didn't believe it. He couldn't.

He got away from them. Rounding a corner, he saw a display case he had somehow missed. In it was a false face mask. It was similar to many others he had seen in ceremonies on the Reserve, with a twisted face and drilled holes for eyes. Its mouth was distorted. It was a modern reproduction, the sign said. Imitation, that meant. It was totally unlike the mask Tom had seen in the bog. That one had been painted red and black, its mouth like two spoons, its eyes bulging and blind. In its empty gaze the power had been deadly real.

Above the imitation mask was an empty space where something had been removed. A small card explained that the mask that belonged there had been taken out by Indian request, because of the mask's "sensitive nature." So that one, like the one in the bog, had been real.

The curator had come then. She was pretty and young and white. They had gone into her office. She had taken the pipe, examining it eagerly, asking him a lot of questions about where he'd found it and when.

He answered her as vaguely as he could and didn't say anything about Laney. When it was over, and she had thanked him, he'd blurted out the thought that was on his mind. "Indians do come here, don't they? Some must, or how would they have asked you to get rid of that other face mask?"

"A few come," she'd said after a pause. "Most of the Indian community is still getting used to the idea of archaeology. They call us grave-diggers, you know." She had shrugged apologetically. "As for the mask we removed from display, apparently it was blessed. We didn't know that when we got it."

"Did they want you to give the blessed mask back to them?"

"Not at all. They just wanted it covered up. They didn't want it lying open on a shelf, even in our warehouse."

Obviously not, Tom thought. A real face mask, exposed to view like that! What he couldn't understand, though, was why they hadn't wanted it back. It was Indian. It was their heritage and full of their magic. Why hadn't they wanted it?

The curator had smiled at him, her long, white fingers running over the pipe. "This is a lovely thing. Too bad the stem is spoiled, but that can't be helped. We'll make sure the pipe gets prominent display. Did you like our museum?"

Our museum. "Oh, yes," he had told her. "Yes, I liked it."

And lying in bed, thinking it all over later, he wished he could have said he hadn't.

After school on Wednesday, Laney saw Tom at her corner, three or four blocks away from his own house. He was kicking absently at a pile of leaves. She wondered what he was doing there.

"Hi," she said. "Did the museum like the pipe?"

"They took it." He shrugged. "Was Hardwick mad, you skipping out yesterday?"

"He couldn't say much. My father wrote me a note."

"Lucky."

"I've got to catch up on all my homework, though," she said, making a face at the load of books in her arms.

"Laney?" he began.

"What?"

How to ask it? He'd already yelled at her once about trying to steal Indian antiquities. If he asked her bluntly about the mask on the body, she'd think he was accusing her again. And what if she hadn't taken it?

"What's up?" Laney asked, seeing his frown.

Maybe there was another way. If it had been Laney who'd taken the mask, she'd have discovered the dead body, too. Maybe he ought to see how she reacted to being told about it.

"You know what else was in the bog that day?" he asked abruptly.

Her thoughts flew to the miniature mask. She licked her lips nervously. "What?"

She was anxious, he saw. That made him say the next thing very loudly. "There was a dead body there." He scanned her face, watching for her reaction.

"A dead—?" Clearly she was astonished. The whites of her eyes shone at him, her voice rising to a squeak. "A person, you mean?"

Tom's shoulders relaxed. It hadn't been she, then. But what about that nervousness of hers a few minutes ago? She had been expecting him to say something else. Not that a body had been in the bog, but that something else had been.

Had she told someone—her archaeologist father, say—about finding the pipe, and had he been the one to go there and take *Gaguwara* away, telling her about it afterward? But would an archaeologist really walk away from an ancient Indian burial and just leave the body to rot?

"Did you call the police about the body?" Laney asked.

He regarded her pityingly. "It was an old burial," he said, "not a murder. Why would I call the police?"

"I don't know. Don't the police always—?" Her voice was shaky. "Tom, you didn't really find a body there, did you?"

"Sure I didn't," he said sarcastically. "That's why I told you I did."

"Laney!" It was Rosemary, yelling at her from the front porch. "Laney, that stupid Hambone's peeing all over Mrs. Easton's roses! She's having a fit!"

"So stop him!" Laney shouted.

"Mrs. Easton's going to call Animal Control. If you want to keep him, you'd better—"

But Laney was gone, running like a deer for Mrs. Easton's house and Hambone.

Mrs. Easton hadn't been going to call Animal Control. She hadn't even threatened it. "Not that I love seeing my rosebed turned into a latrine," she told Laney, "but I like your old Hambone, when he's being good. Just keep him under better control, will you, dear?"

"I'm really sorry," Laney said, while Hambone sat on her feet, his tongue lolling out. "It won't happen again, I promise."

It had been Rosemary who had let him out without a leash, Laney thought furiously, Rosemary who ought to be apologizing, not Laney. And inventing that story about Animal Control! White with anger, Laney went to find her sister. But as usual, she was out. And there'd be no point in complaining to Mom. Mom would just say that if Hambone got to be a nuisance he could always be sold to a Chinese restaurant.

Tom was gone by now, too. Had he really seen a body in the bog? The idea made her sick. She remembered how she'd dug her hands into that mud, feeling for treasure. She'd pulled out the miniature mask, but what if it had been a hand or maybe a nose? She gagged at the thought. No, it couldn't be. Tom must have been kidding her.

But why would he?

"Come on, Hambone," Laney said, clipping on his leash. "We're going for a walk."

It was almost rush hour and busy on Riverside Drive, but she dashed between a car and a truck, dragging Hambone with her. About halfway down the rutted track across the meadow there was a yellow van with its back doors open. Farther on, she saw a couple of men packing up some surveying equipment. It looked as if this time the rumors about the development starting again were true. Hambone growled at the men as they passed, and Laney didn't stop him. If she had been a dog, she'd have done some growling herself.

Now they were alone. The mid-October sky was dark with clouds. A cold wind raced under it, bending the mullein stalks, tossing burdock balls and old leaves, turning stands of dead grass into nets to catch them. Laney's cheeks were scarlet with cold, her curls blown straight back from her face. She shoved her hands into her pockets, trying to warm them. At the edge of the tree-lined slope, where the path led down into the bog, she hesitated for the first time. The path looked dark and uninviting. But she hadn't come all this way just to turn back. She took one step down, then another. Hambone shivered on his leash behind her and didn't even whine to be free. "It's okay, boy," Laney said aloud, to encourage him or maybe herself.

At the trampled-looking bush she remembered, she turned off the main path and pushed her way in. Yes, she could just see the little lime-green pond ahead. The place where she had found the small mask was right at the edge. Probably the body would be there, too. If there was a body at all, she reminded herself.

It was very quiet. The wind had not found its way this far down into the bog. Laney's feet dragged in the mucky soil. Squish, squish, squish. Her eyes were glued to the ground. She didn't want to step on anything. She saw dead branches, a fragile mounding of bog moss, a berry bush the birds were afraid to touch. And then, ahead of her, she saw marks in the mud. Paw prints, they were, and somebody's boots. Other footprints, too, smaller. Her own, from last time? Or Tom's, maybe?

Slower. Slower. She stopped. Tom had not been joking. There was a body in the bog.

Only its face showed, or what was left of it. It was a face that should never have been bared. Laney stared at it. She had thought she would be revolted, but she felt no nausea at all, not even any fear. All she could feel was pity. Had this man once held the little mask that she had found? Had he stroked it, looked into its blind little eyes, sung to it, let it love him?

Had something in him known when she took its protection away?

She was responsible. He was exposed, and she was responsible. Again, snatches of sound drifted into her mind.

He-hawi-yo hawi-yo-ho
he'e waji ha he he we hi he hi ho'o'o

A water drum, deep and slow. He is dead. Keep us safe. Bury him.

The slow shuffle of women, folded arms, bent heads.

he-na-wi'i-yo he-go wi-yo he he

Bury him. Bury his Face. Bury him. And Laney did.

SHE WENT HOME MUDDY AND EXHAUSTED. IT HADN'T been much work, just a few handfuls of earth tossed on that lost and decomposing face, but she felt as if she had dug an entire grave. She got washed, then forced herself to set the table. But then she just sat looking blankly at her homework. The clock ticked. Rosemary came in, yelling about some sausages they were supposed to start before their mother got home from the store. "Did you hear me? I said—"

"The whole world heard you," Laney muttered to herself.

Rosemary threw the sausages into a pan, then slammed on the lid. "Sally Donahue told me Mr. Hardwick kicked you out of class yesterday. She said you were late again." Laney was silent. "I bet you didn't tell Mom."

Laney pushed back her chair. She'd been wondering when Rosemary was going to find out.

"And you missed a test, too."

Laney walked to the door. Over her shoulder she said, "I was only five minutes late. Mr. Hardwick hadn't even finished handing out the questions, but he wouldn't let me take it."

"Sally said you're going to get zero."

Suddenly Laney had had it. "Don't forget to tell Mom," she said. "And, by the way, I skipped school yesterday. You can tell her that, too." And she stalked out.

Rosemary wouldn't quit. She followed Laney down the hall. "Hey, wow, so now you're skipping," she mocked. "You're getting so brave, you might as well be Indian."

"Leave me alone!"

"Must be all those powwows you're having with that Indian kid. Heap big chip on his shoulder Tom Walsh. Everybody's talking about it. My sister, hanging around with a stupid Indian!"

"Tom's got twice as many brains as you and your friends put together!" Laney blazed. She was at the door of her mother's workroom. The door was open, though neither of them noticed.

"Then that's a thousand times as many as you! Nobody decent wants anything to do with Tom Walsh. And nobody decent will have anything to do with you if you keep hanging around him."

"You've got a funny idea of what's decent," Laney said through her teeth.

"I guess you like being a loser."

Loser. Rage rose in Laney, unexpected as a tidal wave. "Shut up!"

"That kid looks dirty. You like people that way? And he's pushy and full of himself and—"

"Shut up!" She almost screamed it. Hate for her sister pounded through her veins. In the room in back of her, something stirred.

"A real item, you two make. Plainy-Laney and Tom the Bomb. God, it makes me want to puke!"

"So go stick your finger down your throat!" Bog mud, thick and black. Violence. "Vomit your guts out! I wish you were de—"

Something stopped her. She never knew what.

For a short, eternal moment Rosemary only stared at her. Then she gulped. "I don't feel very—" she began. She gulped again. Her face went gray. She put her hand to her mouth, her eyes ringed with white. Then she ran to the bathroom. She didn't even have time to shut the door.

"Food poisoning," Dr. Margolin said. "Some bit of junk she ate."

"But nobody else she knows seems to be sick," Alicia McIntyre said. "I've been phoning around." Fred Margolin was an old friend. She'd called him when Rosemary couldn't stop vomiting.

"She must've eaten something no one else had, then," the doctor replied firmly. "You can't always track these things down. Or Rosemary might just have a sensitive gut. Some people do."

"Should she be in a hospital?"

"That's not necessary. Whatever she ate, she's gotten rid of it by now. And I've stopped the vomiting reflex with an injection. She was already half asleep when I left her." He smiled comfortingly. "Give her two of these pills every four hours, and she'll be right as rain by Friday. Now stop worrying."

Mrs. McIntyre saw him out into the night. Laney was on the living room sofa, head to knees, making herself small. It was almost ten o'clock, and she was very tired. Outside, rain fell, a steady drumming. "Thanks again, Fred!" Mrs. McIntyre called. A car started up. The door slammed.

Food poisoning. Well, of course. What else could it have been?

"That's a relief," Mrs. McIntyre said, coming back into the room. She yawned. "God, I'm exhausted."

She had been the one to stand with Rosemary during the bouts of nausea, stroking the sick girl's hair, wiping her face gently, not even showing any revulsion. Laney had tried to help, but Rosemary only pulled away. Laney didn't blame her. *Vomit your guts out!* She could still hear herself screaming it. And then, hour after hour, Rosemary almost had.

"You should be in bed, Laney," Mom said. She took a sip of the tea Laney had brought her. She didn't notice it was cold.

Food poisoning, Laney thought again. Dr. Margolin was positive that was it.

"I don't know how I'm going to stay up till two to give her these pills," her mother said, stretching.

"I'll do it," Laney offered.

"You've got school in the morning. But thanks." She yawned again.

"You've got work. Anyway, I had a nap after school," Laney lied. "I'm not even tired."

"It's nice of you, darling. I know you mean it, but—"

"Really, Mom, I can do it. You go to bed."

"Well, maybe I'll just take a little nap. You'll wake me when you get tired?"

"Sure."

Her mother stood up. "You've been a big help tonight, Laney." She smiled, a gentle smile that would have made Laney's heart expand if she had felt less wretched. A help, she thought. She shivered.

But it wasn't she who'd caused Rosemary's sickness. It was just a coincidence, Rosemary getting so sick after what she had said. It had to have been!

The hours passed. Laney turned on the television, but she didn't watch it. Instead she did homework, pouring all her concentration into it, not letting herself think of the workroom down the hall or of the silence in the house that the TV couldn't hide. At two she took the pills into Rosemary's room.

In the light from the hall Rosemary's sleeping face looked ashen. Hesitantly, Laney stood over her. At last she shook her gently. Rosemary's eyes fluttered open. "Take these," Laney whispered to her, holding out the pills and a glass of water. Rosemary swallowed the pills, still half asleep. Then, slowly, awareness returned to her eyes, and doubt.

"Where's Mom?" she asked, drawing away.

"In bed. Rosemary, I'm sorry you were so sick."

"Sure. 'Puke your guts out,' that's what you said. Right?" She was trying for her old scorn, but there was too much uncertainty in her voice.

"Anyway, I'm sorry. Dr. Margolin said you had food poisoning."

"Pretty funny, me getting so sick right after you—"

"It was a coincidence."

"Funny kind of coincidence. Remind me to laugh." And she turned her face to the wall. Laney's hands gripped one another tightly. Then she left the room. Down the hall her mother's workroom door was still open. Laney hesitated on the threshold, not turning on the light. She didn't have to. She could feel the mask inside. She knew it was watching her. Chewing her lip, she closed the door tightly. There was no way to lock it, but she wished there were.

Rosemary seemed better the next day, and Mrs. McIntyre arranged for Lorna Easton to come in while she went to work. Laney got to school on time. She sat rigid through her classes, paying attention as she never had before, closing her mind to anything but what her teachers were saying. She handed in her homework before anyone asked her. She kept her eyes down in science and gym and ate her lunch outside by herself. She hurried home right after school. It was one of the hardest days she had ever spent.

"How's Rosemary?" she asked Mrs. Easton before she'd even taken off her jacket.

"Running me ragged." Mrs. Easton gave a mock grimace. "Turn her pillows, make her some soup, get her some lemonade, and can she please have the TV in her room? On the mend, I'd definitely say." She smiled. "Take her this toast, will you, dear?"

The plate of toast shook as Laney entered her sister's room. "Hi," she said nervously, holding out the toast.

"Hi." Rosemary's eyes were cool, but there was none of last night's uncertainty in them.

"You feeling better?"

"I'll live." She took the toast. "If I don't starve to death, that is."

Laney watched while she ate a piece. "You look better," she said at last.

"I look like something from under a rock. God, that must've been some rotten burger I ate yesterday. I thought it tasted funny."

"You did?" Laney said eagerly.

"Did Web ask about me today?"

"I didn't see him."

"You never see anybody." Rosemary shook her head. "You live in the clouds, or what?"

Back to normal, then. That, too, was a relief.

Laney took Hambone for a quick walk down to the river, then spent an hour at the kitchen table with her homework. She saved her math till last. The calculator made it so easy, she could almost look forward to it. Tonight's homework was on the order of operations. Brackets, exponents, multiplying, and adding, all mixed up in the same question. Hard stuff, and negatives to worry about, too. She worked it out on the calculator in bits, then got the final answer to each question. Then she checked the answers at the back. All correct, as usual. She almost closed the book, but then something hit her. The fraction part, yes, that the calculator had done. But it had been *she* who'd figured out what order to do everything in and where the signs went. And the answers were all correct, which meant she had done her part right!

Wow, she thought wonderingly. Thirty-five questions, and every single one right. Was she actually starting to understand math?

Mrs. McIntyre came in then. "Rosemary's fine," Laney said happily.

"I know." Her mother smiled. "I talked to Lorna." She saw the calculator on the kitchen table. "That looks expensive," she said, still smiling. "Where'd you get it?"

Other than a direct lie, there was no way out. "Dad got it for me," she said. Mrs. McIntyre's smile didn't fade, but somehow it changed. "I—well, I've been doing pretty awful in math. Dad thought if I got this, it might take some of the pressure off. That way I might get to understand it without—"

"Your father," Alicia said, "is an expert at taking the pressure off. Why do you think he's only an associate professor, after all these years?" She picked up the calculator and examined it. "When did he give it to you?"

Laney looked down. "Tuesday," she muttered.

"That's not your day to see him."

"I met him by accident. On a bus."

"I see." She was still looking at the calculator. "Did you know he hasn't had a grant in years, Laney? And that the only papers he writes are about other people's finds? He's got tenure, of course; otherwise he might not even have a job. I've heard that some of his colleagues laugh at him."

Laney said nothing. Her mother looked up. "Does Mr. Hardwick let you use calculators on your tests?" she asked coolly.

Stricken, Laney stared at her. The thought had never occurred to her.

"I'll bet he doesn't." Mrs. McIntyre tossed the calculator into Laney's lap. "You'd better keep that in mind while this thing gets all your homework right for you. Sooner or later, you're going to have to do the work without it."

And then she went to look after Rosemary.

SITTING A LITTLE APART FROM THE REST OF THE CLASS, Tom was painting. On Wednesday, when Mrs. James had assigned this project, all it had been going to be was a color study. Different shades of two colors only, Mrs. James had said. Tom had started without any colors in mind, or any particular image. By Thursday he had known he would use tones of charcoal and red. By Friday, he was painting the mask.

He hadn't intended to do it. He had seen the mask only once. He didn't even want to remember it. But it was as if he had no choice in the matter. Slash, splash, sweep, went the paint onto the canvas. And out came the roughness of preserved wood, the grainy bits of black and red, the straggly hair surmounting those great, gaping eyes. He was immersed in it. He had unearthed the mask and lost it. Now he was finding it again.

He didn't see the woman visitor come in. He didn't even notice when she stopped by his table, silently watching. "Clean up, now, everyone," Mrs. James called, but he didn't hear. He was almost finished. Just a few more strokes . . . The school bell shrilled the class change, but he didn't hear that, either.

Mrs. James shook him gently by the shoulder. He blinked up at her, then looked back at his painting. It was done, and it was good. That was all that mattered.

"It's marvelous, Tom," Mrs. James said, staring at the painting. "I've never seen anything so evil."

The other woman, whom he noticed now for the first time, said, "Not all of it's evil, though. See that brush stroke there, and the ones by the eyes? They're almost gentle. I like that."

Tom looked at her with respect. She was an old woman and white, but she had understood.

"This is Jane Collingwood, Tom," Mrs. James said.

Tom blinked. Jane Collingwood was a famous painter. Mrs. James had talked about her only last week. What was she doing here, in the ninth-grade art class at Riverview?

"I'm collecting young people's art for a new national gallery in Ottawa," the visitor explained. "Mrs. James wrote to me about you, Tom. I came to see your work."

"*My* work?" Tom shook himself.

"Mrs. James has been showing me your other things. They're all good, but this mask is the best. Would you let me exhibit it in the gallery?"

The late bell rang. Tom turned away, wiping his brush, tidying his bench. The mask, on display. He hadn't meant to paint it. He certainly hadn't meant for anyone besides Mrs. James to see it. And now someone wanted to put it up in a gallery for white people to gawk at. He couldn't allow it; that was clear.

Still, it was good. He knew it was good. Pride stirred in him. But it was a white pride. It made the Indian part of him ashamed.

"I can't," he told the visitor, and because she had understood the painting, added, "It's something—private."

She nodded thoughtfully. "All good art—Indian or white—is private. That's what makes it good." She handed him a card. "I won't try to persuade you," she added, "but if you should change your mind, here is my address."

With a late slip clutched in one hand and the artist's card in the other, Tom went to his next class. He sat through it blank-eyed, not taking in a single thing. By Tom Walsh, he thought. His name up there in Ottawa, for everyone to see. He liked the thought. Did he ever like it! But if he had been completely Indian, he wouldn't have liked it at all. He would have been too shocked at the idea of displaying the mask even to be tempted.

He looked at the window and saw a reflection of his face: the high ridge of his cheekbones, the rounded jaw, the straight black hair, the darkness. Pure Indian, he thought. Nothing white about him at all. His eyes stared back at him, knowing the lie, accusing him.

He turned away. Why, he thought miserably, why had his mother brought him here?

By Saturday morning Rosemary was her old self again. She pounded on the bathroom door for Laney to get out, then spent an hour showering and putting on her makeup. She came into the kitchen looking like a rock star. Alicia McIntyre was sitting over her coffee and newspaper, while Laney combed Hambone.

"Can I have some money, Mom?" Rosemary asked, pulling out her chair.

Her mother gave her a wry look. "And good morning to you, too, Madonna."

Rosemary grinned. "It'll be a better one if you give me the money."

"How much?" Alicia said succinctly, though her mouth twitched.

"How much ya got, baby?" Rosemary asked out of the corner of her mouth, aping the gangster movie they'd watched on TV the night before.

Mrs. McIntyre laughed and reached for her purse. I might as well not be here, Laney thought. She wanted to talk; she wanted to be part of it all. But she simply couldn't think of a thing to say. Tugging on a mat of fur behind Hambone's ear, she pretended not to mind. Why was it always so easy between Mom and Rosemary? Why couldn't *she* be comfortable with Mom, like that?

It was a beautiful day, bright and warm for October.

A breeze from the open window stirred a pile of Hambone's loose fur. Some of it drifted Rosemary's way. "*Do* you mind?" she asked Laney pointedly. "Dog fur's not exactly my favorite breakfast."

"Must you comb that dog in the kitchen?" Mrs. McIntyre said.

Laney gathered up the fur and threw it away. Rosemary was reading the entertainment section. Alicia was going through the local news. "Well, well," she said suddenly. "Your father's made the newspaper."

"What for?" Laney asked, coming over.

"It's that bog of yours. Apparently the developer's been surveying in the meadow again. Your father's getting up on his soapbox—"

"He's always up on a soapbox," Rosemary said, bored.

"—his usual thing about how there may have been an important Indian settlement in the area, how it was bad enough to destroy the ecology, blah, blah, without wrecking our heritage, blah, blah, blah." Mrs. McIntyre made a face. "He's been talking for years about an Indian settlement over there. And no proof at all that Indians ever even came here."

"But—" Laney began, thinking of the miniature mask and the Indian pipe and comb. Mom knew about those. Weren't they proof that Indians had been here?

"And does he ever do any digging to prove his theories?" Mom went on. "Oh, no. Not on private land without permission. Instead he sounds off in the newspaper. The resident expert without a find to his name."

"That's not fair," Laney muttered. Mom was flipping pages, and Rosemary was yawning. Neither of them heard her.

Ashamed, she left the room. Hambone followed her out. "I should have said something, shouldn't I, boy?" she said, when they were out in the clean air. "Why am I so gutless?"

Hambone nuzzled her lovingly. It was almost as if he knew.

The light was on in the workroom, and the door was open. Laney stopped in the hall, looking in. Almost suppertime on a Saturday night, and still her mother was bent over her workbench. The goldfish bowl was empty.

"Where's the mask?" Laney blurted out, before she could think.

Her mother looked up. "I'm working on it."

"Doing what?"

"Changing the percentage of alcohol in the solution."

"But where is it?" She had to know.

Mrs. McIntyre jerked her head toward a wrapped bundle on the bench in front of her. "What's the matter, did you think I'd sold it already?"

"No, I—well—"

"It's got another week in chemicals before it can go on the shelf," Mrs. McIntyre said.

Laney imagined the little mask with a price tag on it. It gave her the courage to say the next thing, the thing she'd been thinking all day. "That mask's got to be proof the Indians came here," she said. "Why don't you show it to Dad? It might help him stop the devel—"

"Absolutely not. *Neither* of us will show it to your father. Neither of us will even mention it. Do I make myself clear?"

"But why?"

"Because," Mrs. McIntyre said deliberately, "you broke the law by removing that mask from its location without informing the archaeologists. Your father would feel he should make an example out of you. You don't want to have to go to court, do you?"

Tom had taken the pipe to the Indian museum, Laney thought, and no one there had tried to prosecute him for removing it from the spot where it was found. If they hadn't, why would Dad do it to his own daughter?

There was something too straight about her mother's eyes. "I'm not the one who'd go to court," Laney said slowly, understanding dawning. "It's you. Selling it would be breaking the law. That's why you don't want Dad to know, isn't it? Because you want to sell it, and you know it's illegal."

Her mother's eyes narrowed. Then she gave a little shrug. "Fair enough. But think for a minute, before you get all holier-than-thou. Ten thousand dollars, Laney. Maybe even more."

"I don't care about the money," Laney said miserably.

Her mother's lips tightened. "You don't need to, do you? You're living under a roof I pay for, eating food I buy, wearing clothes I give you. Of course you don't care about money! Now you listen to me, Laney McIntyre. I *am* going to sell this mask, and your father *would* prosecute me if he knew. So you just keep it in mind. If you want to see me go before a judge, you tell your father about that mask. If you like the status quo around here, keep your mouth shut. That's all there is to it."

Her eyes glittered at Laney like polished blue stones. "Mom," Laney pleaded. Suddenly she couldn't bear it. Anything was better than having Mom look at her like that. "I won't tell Dad," she whispered. "I promise."

Slowly, the blue gaze softened. "I didn't really think you would." Then, almost gently, she added, "The money's not just for me, you know. It's for all of us. A down payment on that summer cottage we've always wanted. Piano lessons for you and Rosemary. Some pretty new clothes, maybe." She brushed Laney's cheek with a cool kiss. "You're doing the right thing, darling. You'll see."

Laney hugged her mother anxiously. It was like hugging wood. "Now run along," Alicia said. "I've got to get this job finished. Tell Rosemary supper will be in an hour, will you?"

She was already unwrapping the mask. Laney backed away, but not before the little face came to light. Black for hate, red for love, the thin, thin line dividing the two . . .

Tears blinded her. She fled.

IT WAS STILL VERY EARLY. A SUNDAY QUIET FILLED THE air. All over old South London, behind the big front verandas and the gables and shutters, other people were sleeping. Laney stood in front of the house where her father lived. She had taken the bus, then walked the last few blocks because it was so early. Dad wouldn't expect her to arrive before breakfast. Actually, he wouldn't be expecting her at all. On their Sundays together Dr. McIntyre always came to pick her up.

Laney had been awake before dawn. In the week since she had found the little mask, she had not slept properly. Either she would toss and turn late into the night or wake up far too early, desperate for sleep, but thinking and worrying instead. She didn't know exactly what she was afraid of, only that it had something to do with the mask. Today the feeling had been worse than ever, a nasty, creeping apprehension, like rats in the house. Unable to face it, she had dressed and left the house before anyone else was awake.

At the last moment, about to go out the door, she

had gone back to her room to get the antler comb. Unlike the mask, Mom hadn't made her promise not to tell Dad about it. Laney still wasn't sure she was going to let her father see it. If she did, Dad would want to know exactly where she'd found it, and somehow she couldn't bear it if that body in the bog were dug up again. Still, the comb was Indian and old. It would prove to Dad that he was right about there being an ancient Indian settlement near the bog. It might even get him permission to do a dig.

Her mother's scornful voice echoed in her mind: *Without a find to his name,* she had said. And: *They laugh at him.*

Dr. McIntyre had four small rooms on the top floor of a house that was almost a hundred years old. The side door was a common entrance for all the tenants and wasn't kept locked. Laney loitered outside until just after eight, then went in and up the stairs. Nervously she knocked on her father's door.

"Why, Laney!"

Her father was still in his pajamas, his light brown hair all rumpled from sleep. But there was no anger in his eyes.

"I'm sorry to come. So early, I mean. I mean—"

"I was up," Dr. McIntyre said calmly. "Come in. I'll make us some hot chocolate."

She had forgotten that about Dad. Hot chocolate in the morning, never coffee. And then, on Sundays while Mom slept in, he would take Rosemary and Laney to the Portuguese bakery. She followed her father into the kitchen. Books and papers were stacked in neat piles on the table. He cleared a space for her. "Sit down," he said, busying himself at the counter. "How's the calculator working?"

"Fine," Laney said. Then, uncomfortably, "Mr. Hardwick doesn't let us use them on tests, though."

"We didn't get it for you for tests." Her father turned on the stove and put a pot on the burner. Then he sat down beside Laney. "Have you thought what you'd like to do today?"

That was something else she'd forgotten. Dad didn't push. He might be wondering if the calculator was making her more relaxed about doing math on her own, but Laney knew he wouldn't ask. He probably wouldn't even ask why she was here so early today. She made herself think about his question. What did she want to do today? "It's really nice out," she said tentatively. "Could we do something outside?"

"No movies?" Dr. McIntyre asked, quirking his brows at her.

"I don't really like watching TV all day," she admitted. There, it was out. She was amazed how easy it had been.

"When you were little," he replied, "we couldn't pry you away from *Sesame Street.*" He poured their cocoa. "People change, though. Rosemary used to love Portuguese rolls. Now I suppose she wouldn't touch them."

They drank for a few moments in silence. "Something outside," her father repeated. Then, tentatively, "One of my students, John Hamilton, has a dig going on in the woods near Delaware. He'll probably be there by ten or so. But I don't suppose you'd enjoy—"

"Is it an Indian settlement?"

"A Neutral hunting camp, actually. It's quite interesting. There're a lot of artifacts."

"Any false face masks?" Laney asked before she could stop herself.

Her father smiled. "That would be some find in a Neutral camp! Where did you hear about false faces?"

"In a book somewhere," Laney said evasively. "What did you mean, that'd be some find?"

"It was the Iroquois who had Medicine Societies and false face masks, not the Neutrals."

"I thought the Neutrals were Iroquois, too."

"They lived an Iroquois way of life. You know, living in longhouses, that sort of thing? But they didn't have false face masks. Or, at least, there has never been any evidence that they did." He grinned, his face alive with enthusiasm. "This whole area was Neutral territory. If John Hamilton managed to find a false face here, he'd go down in archaeological history. But he won't, unfortunately. The Neutrals were pretty well dispersed by 1650 or so, and even if they did have False Face Societies, wooden masks simply don't last three hundred years. Not buried in ordinary earth."

But bogs weren't ordinary earth. Laney's fingers clenched on her cup. "London was Neutral territory, too?" she asked carefully. "All of it? Our bog, too?"

"That's right."

He went on then, telling her more about the Neutral Indians, but Laney wasn't listening. A false face on a Neutral site. That was what she had found. And she'd taken it away, and Mom was going to sell it. And now no one would ever know that the Neutrals had had Medicine Societies. No one would go down in archaeological history because of it.

Conscience stricken, she chewed her lip. But she had promised—*she had promised!*—not to tell. Her hand went into her pocket. "Dad," she said abruptly, stopping him in midsentence.

"Yes?" He saw what she was holding out. "Good heavens, Laney, where did you get this?" He took the comb from her gently, his eyes excited.

"Hambone found it in the bog," she said evasively.

"The bog? Across from our house, you mean?" She nodded. "It's Neutral, definitely," he said, his hands caressing it.

"Does it mean there's a settlement there?"

"Well, not there," he replied, still running his fingers over it. "Nobody ever lives in a bog. It might have been dropped by accident, by some hunter, perhaps. A bog was a great place for hunting, in those days. And a hunter might have come there from anywhere."

"Then you couldn't use the comb to prove there

was a settlement in the meadow, say?" she asked, disappointed.

"I wish I could. I've wondered all my adult life if one's over there. There used to be a grand little stream cutting across the meadow, then forking just before it dropped into the bog. The area between the forks would have been a perfect spot for a settlement: fertile, a good supply of fresh water, easily defended. I've asked the owner five or six times to let me dig there, but he's always refused."

"You couldn't just dig there on your own?"

"Oh, I could dig," her father said. "The trouble is, nothing found in an illegal dig could ever be made public. And even if it could, I wouldn't do it. There are very strict professional rules about having to get permission for digs, you see. And I happen to believe in those rules. What if someone tore up my basement floor without asking me because he thought he might find an Indian burial there? Just because the rules are inconvenient for me now doesn't mean I should break them." He turned abruptly away, putting dishes in the sink.

He hadn't mentioned Laney's mother, but she was there all the same, standing between them, her face scornful.

Dr. McIntyre finished stacking the dishes. "What are you going to do with the comb?" he asked.

"Mom said it isn't very valuable."

"Value isn't always measured in dollars and cents, especially when something can't be sold anyway." His eyes had turned cold. "Selling antiquities is illegal, you know. I wouldn't like to think anyone I knew was engaging in it."

She struggled for a casual look. So Mom had been right. Dad would prosecute her if he found out she was selling the little mask. "I wouldn't have sold the comb," she said.

"I know *you* wouldn't."

"I just thought I might keep it. I—like it."

Slowly, warmly, her father smiled. "I like it, too," he said.

"Should it go to a museum?"

Dr. McIntyre was silent for a long moment. Then, surprisingly, he said, "I don't think there's any hurry about it. Keep it till you're ready. After that it can go on the shelf, where nobody but the cleaners will ever touch it again." He shrugged. "Sometimes I wonder why we put everything behind glass. It's one thing if an artifact is unique, but with something as common as this, why not let kids like you handle it, feel what it was like to be the person who used it every day? It'd be a change from learning history from the textbooks."

"That's a funny thing for an archaeologist to say," Laney got out.

"Maybe I'm a funny archaeologist," her father said

wryly. "Now are we going to John Hamilton's dig, or are we going to the bakery?"

"Why not both?" Laney said simply.

It was after dark by the time she got home, tired, dirty, and happy. John Hamilton had assumed they'd come to help, and after only a little instruction Laney had taken over the sifting from him, putting piles of soil through the giant screen and picking out rocks and twigs, then looking hopefully at what remained. All on her own she'd identified two arrowheads and a scraper. The excitement remained even after saying good-bye to her father, but coming into the house she forgot everything. From the kitchen she could hear the sound of Hambone yipping.

She ran down the hall. In the kitchen Hambone was cowering in the corner by an overturned garbage pail. His snout showed traces of last night's leftovers. Alicia McIntyre had a rolled-up newspaper in her hand and was hitting him. There was a look on her face Laney had never seen before.

"You stupid animal! Look at this mess! I hope that garbage makes you sick." She hit him again, harder and harder, again and again and again. Hambone had his tail between his legs, and his yip was turning into little yelps of pain.

"You're hurting him!" Laney cried, rushing forward and grabbing her mother's arm.

"Will you look at this mess? Look at it! Eating garbage, for God's sake! Bad dog. Bad, bad dog!" And she shook Laney free, raising the newspaper again.

"No. *No!*" Again Laney grabbed her arm. "Mom, I'll clean everything up. Leave him alone, Mom. You're acting like you want to kill him!"

"Kill him!" Her mother stared at her. "Don't be ridiculous." Her arm dropped. The newspaper fell to the floor. "Good heavens, can't you tell the difference between a little discipline and—?"

But it hadn't been just a little discipline. Laney stared at her mother. "His bowls are empty," she whispered. "Did anybody feed him today?"

"Didn't you?" Alicia asked, straightening her hair.

"He's starving. No wonder he—"

"A couple of missed meals is hardly an excuse for raiding the garbage," her mother said. But her voice wasn't nearly as calm as her words. Half to herself she added, "I did hit him a lot."

Hambone was shivering in the corner, staring at Mrs. McIntyre like a sick rabbit caught by a fox. Suddenly, he vomited. "Eating garbage," Mrs. McIntyre said, raising her chin to hide the strain in her eyes. "Serves him right."

She left the room. Laney ran to Hambone. "It's all right, boy," she whispered, rubbing his ears, trying to reassure him. "It's all right."

But it wasn't, and they all knew it.

Hambone was sick so many times that Laney called the veterinary emergency number. "He'll stop when he's got rid of whatever's bothering him," the technician said. "But bring him in if you're worried."

How could she, without asking her mother? A taxi? She didn't have enough money. And if she asked Dad, Mom would never forgive her.

She sat up with Hambone, bathing his face, keeping him warm. There was nothing left in him to bring up, and still he kept retching. It was just like the other night, Laney thought, only it wasn't Rosemary this time. *I hope that garbage makes you sick:* Mom's voice. And the other night, her own: *Vomit your guts out.* And they had. They did. She threw her arms around Hambone, willing him to be well. And at two in the morning, when she was exhausted and Hambone was so sick she couldn't bear it anymore and there was nothing else she could think of, she went to her mother's workroom.

The mask faced her. It wasn't I, the blind eyes seemed to say. It wasn't I, not this time.

"Then make him well," she said. "Please, please, make him well!"

She stared at it, at the warm red side, not the black; at those sightless, knowing, powerful eyes. Suddenly a great calm filled her. She went back to the kitchen and stroked Hambone's quivering muzzle. "Be well, boy," she whispered. And the peace in her went into him, and he gave her finger a tiny lick. Then tired out, they fell asleep together.

SHE WOKE JUST AFTER DAWN WITH HAMBONE LICKING her face. He woofed softly when he saw she was awake, then went to his food dish and nudged it. "You're hungry," Laney said. "Oh, Hambone, that's great!" She got to her feet, cramped muscles protesting, and half-filled his bowl. He wolfed it down, then looked pleadingly at her for more.

"Not right now," she said, patting him, "not till we're sure that's going to stay down." She smiled at his injured expression. "If you're back to being Robert Redford again, you must be all right."

She waited five minutes, then gave him some more. After he had eaten that, and drunk a little, he seemed tired again. She threw on a jacket and took him outside. The dawn sky was pale and cold. While she waited for Hambone to finish, a leaf drifted softly onto her head. There weren't many of them left now. And it was cold, too, cold enough to make her shiver, even in her warm jacket. Her breath wreathed her face. "Come on, boy," she called him. "You're not staying outside today."

She took him to her room. It wasn't allowed, but she didn't care. She wanted Hambone comfortable, and she wanted him to feel safe. And she was pretty sure her mother would be glad enough not to see him, anyway. Hambone chose a protected corner inside her closet, and Laney wrapped him in her old comforter. She left his water dish beside him, propped open the door, and threw herself down on the bed.

It was too late now for sleep. It didn't matter. She wasn't tired; not in her mind, anyway. It felt wide awake, sharp and transparent as crystal. Thoughts shone through from one layer to another, building on one another, evolving. Mingled with them on every level was her mother's face, her cool, beautiful looks solidified to an unforgettable ugliness, a mask of power and rage.

Out of control, Laney thought. Mom, who never hit anyone, who always had control over every situation she was in, had acted as if she had wanted to kill Hambone, and all for the sake of a little spilled garbage.

And only a few days ago, for the sake of a minor insult, Laney had acted as if she wanted to kill Rosemary.

All since the mask came into the house, the mask that Indians could use to harm as well as to heal. Was there a connection? Could there be?

She pictured the mask, its pain-filled face, half black, half red. If it did have power, if somehow Laney had plugged into it that time Rosemary had gotten sick, and if her mother had done the same thing last night—

She remembered Rosemary baiting her, the workroom door open at her back, the feel of something in there, readying itself to obey her command. *Her* command. The truth of it struck at her suddenly. The little mask was hers, not her mother's at all. Even the books said that a mask belonged to only one person. If the little mask could obey anyone, it would be Laney, who had taken the mask from the bog and made it hers. Not her mother, who had ill-wished Hambone, but Laney, who had wished him better.

And he had gotten better.

Could the mask actually be magical? Had it cured Hambone and hurt Rosemary, just because Laney had wished it? Were its black and red halves like something evil and something good existing together?

A power to be used, Laney thought. A choice.

If she had known Rosemary would get sick, would she have wished it anyway?

There was no escaping the questions. And the only answer that seemed clear was that it couldn't have been Mrs. McIntyre's ill wish that had caused Hambone's illness. Even supposing the little mask was magical—and that possibility was something Laney didn't want to admit—its magic simply wasn't Mom's to command. Hambone must've just gotten sick because he was scared and had eaten garbage.

So why didn't she believe it?

Danger. They were all in danger. In the warmth of

her bed Laney felt suddenly cold. She shook herself, got up, made a neat pile of yesterday's clothes. Feelings were only feelings. It was time to get ready for school.

Mom was sitting over her coffee. "Good morning, Laney," she said pleasantly.

"Morning," Laney replied, trying for her mother's calm.

"Cereal or eggs?" Mom asked.

Laney shook her head. She wasn't hungry.

"Some toast, then," her mother said firmly. She got to her feet. "Hambone over his upset stomach?" she asked casually, putting some bread in the toaster.

"He's fine." She drank her milk, keeping her eyes down.

"I've been wondering about putting the garbage can under the sink where he can't get at it. What do you think? Will he just invent some other terrible sin if we do?" Alicia smiled at her, inviting her to smile in return. She was in a good mood, Laney thought in amazement. How could she be, after last night?

To Laney's relief Rosemary came in. Under her spiky blond hair her face might have been a Sears model's. She was wearing a pale blue sweater of her mother's. It exactly matched the color of her eyes. "Good morning, Rosemary," Mrs. McIntyre said, her eyebrows quirked. "That's a nice sweater you're wearing."

Rosemary grinned. "Perfect fit, huh?"

"Lucky for you I'm celebrating," Mrs. McIntyre said. "I just heard some great news. Listen to this. Bronwyn's is finished."

Bronwyn's was the oldest antique store in London. Ever since Heritage Lane had opened, it had been Mrs. McIntyre's chief competition. "I heard it on the radio this morning," Mom went on. Her voice was excited. "This is the break I've been waiting for. The old man's closing the place right down, not even selling it! So where do you think all his customers will go?"

"Heritage Lane, where else?" Rosemary said, raising clasped hands over her head in a victory sign. "We're gonna be rich!"

Her mother laughed. "Hardly that. But I was thinking, what would you two say to Miami this Christmas?"

"Can we make it Lauderdale instead?" Rosemary asked.

"Why not? I'll call a travel agent this morning and see." Absently she put Laney's toast down in front of Rosemary.

"Why is Mr. Bronwyn closing, Mom?" Laney asked.

Her mother shrugged. "How should I know? Maybe he just got tired."

Tired of being the most successful antique dealer in London? Well, it was possible. But if the store was as profitable as Mom always said, Mr. Bronwyn could have made a lot of money selling it. And instead he had just closed down. By doing that, he'd made Heritage

Lane the most important antique store in the city. Laney looked at her mother and tried to feel glad.

Tom waited for Laney after science class on Monday. Last night he had dreamed that someone was wearing the mask from the bog. Nothing had happened, nothing bad; he had wakened too soon. But he was sweating, the same way he sweated in horror movies just before the evil thing walked in. This morning he was doubly sure that he must find out where the mask had gone, and that there was no time to be lost.

"I've got to talk to you," he told Laney. "It's important."

She looked at him in surprise, the rush of students passing them by. "Okay, sure." She waited.

"Not here," Tom said. "How about meeting me somewhere after school?"

"I have to go right home. Hambone was sick last night. What's this all about, anyway?"

"A mask," Tom said briefly, and had the satisfaction of seeing her face tighten. So she did know something about it, he thought grimly.

"I—we could talk at lunch, maybe."

Tom tried to imagine it, his grilling her about the mask in front of the whole cafeteria. "No way," he said. "This is private."

"You could walk home with me," she suggested, flushing a little. A boy and a girl walking home together meant something. "Or you could come over to my house."

"I'll meet you somewhere," he said coolly.

All day Laney thought about it. How did Tom know she'd taken the little mask from the bog? And what would he expect her to do about it? After school she took her usual route home, though a little faster than usual. He showed up about halfway home, joining her from a side street.

"Do you know who took that mask off the body?" he asked, without even a greeting.

"I did," Laney said, in a low, guilty voice. "I had it in my hand when you showed up at the bog that day. I put it in my pocket, and you didn't notice."

"You put it in your—?"

"I didn't know what it was then. I hadn't had a chance to look at it. You were being such a pig about the pipe, I just hid it in my hand, and—"

"Why are you lying? Are you trying to protect someone?"

Laney flushed indignantly. "I'm telling you the truth!"

"The truth! You're lying your head off. Hiding a full-sized mask in your hand. Putting it in your pocket!"

Laney's eyes widened. "A full-sized mask! But that's not—the one I found wasn't—Tom, it was tiny! A miniature!"

They had stopped walking. "A miniature," Tom repeated dazedly. "But it can't have been. It—"

His thoughts swam. He had seen miniature masks before, tied to the hair of the larger false faces. They protected the owner against the magic of the full-sized masks. Sometimes they worked magic of their own. But if the mask Laney had found was a miniature, who had taken the large one that had been on the face of the body?

"I can show it to you," Laney said. "It's in my mom's workroom. She's preserving it. It isn't a full-sized mask; I swear it isn't!"

"The one I saw was. It was covering the face of that body. And now it's gone."

A second mask. And she had thought one was trouble! "Well, someone else took it, then, not me."

"Who?"

"I don't know." She lifted her chin. "It could've been anybody."

"I only left it there for a day. From Sunday, when I dug it up, to Monday after school. And hardly anyone goes into that part of the bog."

"You did. And I did. Anybody might have—"

"You said your mother was preserving the miniature mask?"

"She—well, it would rot if she didn't."

"She's an antique dealer, isn't she? Does she want to sell it?" Silence. "If she knew where it was found, maybe she would have gone there to see if there was anything else worth selling. Did you show her where you'd found the little mask?" Silence. "Well, did you?"

"No." Defiantly. "No, I didn't."

She hadn't shown her. But she had told her, Laney thought miserably. She had described the location very, very carefully. And later Mom had gone out. In rubber boots.

Tom was watching her carefully. He knew there was something she wasn't saying. "Do you know anything about what those masks can do?" he asked intensely.

"I've read about them. They're supposed to be able to cure sickness. Sometimes they even cause it. I don't see how they can, though."

"You don't have to see," Tom said. "They don't care what you think. They're just—powerful. They like power. And they don't like to be controlled."

"Why're you telling me all this?"

"So you'll know what you're responsible for."

"I'm not responsible for anything."

He looked at her scornfully. "Listen to this, Miss Not My Fault. As soon as that mask was taken off the body, it changed ownership. Whoever took it now owns it till he's dead, or till he gives it up willingly to someone else. Owning a false face can be really dangerous, even to an Indian. That's why miniature masks were made in the first place, to control the large ones and to protect the owner from them."

"So?"

"So if something bad happens to the person who took the large mask, or to the people he or she doesn't like, who do you think will have caused it?"

"All I did was take the miniature mask! I didn't even know there was a large one!"

"Yeah, but because I saw you with your hands in the bog, I dug up the large mask," Tom said grimly. "We're both responsible, Laney McIntyre. And we're going to stay responsible until we get those masks back where they belong. So we're going to have to find that large mask. You and I. Both of us. And we're going to have to persuade the owner to give it back to us, or sell it to us, if it takes every penny we've got. And after that, we're going to have to get the little one away from your mother."

"She'll never give it to me," Laney whispered.

"She won't have to. Who took it from the body? You did. So who do you think it belongs to? Who's it going to protect? Who's it going to give power to?"

Me, Laney thought. It's going to protect me. It's going to give me power.

She had known it all along.

HAMBONE GREETED HER AT THE DOOR, TRAILING HER COMforter behind him. No one else was home. Laney spent a few minutes with the big, yellow dog, checking him over, feeding him, putting him out. He seemed to be perfectly all right again. The hours and hours of sickness might never have happened at all. A magical recovery, Laney said to herself. It wasn't a comforting thought.

She went into the kitchen and drank a glass of water. After that she set the table, turned on the oven and put in the roast, and went back out into the living room, where she plumped up three pillows and put away a book. But none of it was any good. She simply couldn't stop thinking of the masks.

Had her mother gone to the bog that day and taken away the big mask? Had it been the large mask, not the small one, that had fulfilled Mom's ill wish and made Hambone sick? Was it down the hall in her workroom right now, hidden away, being preserved in chemicals?

Laney wished Rosemary would come home. The

house was too quiet, too full of possibilities. Laney didn't want to go into the workroom. She didn't want to search for the big mask. But she knew she was going to have to if Rosemary didn't come home soon. She wouldn't be able to stop herself.

The minutes ticked by, and Rosemary didn't come. Laney thought about putting on her coat and going downtown. But it was too late. She was already at the workroom door.

In the fishbowl the little mask was surrounded by bubbles. Laney thought of a diver exhaling slowly under water. She forced her eyes away. There was a bank of cupboards above the table, and she opened them one by one, standing on a stool to search. The large mask would be easy to find if it was here. It was big and must be in an even bigger chemical bath.

Under the empty gaze of the miniature mask Laney looked in all the cupboards, and even in the desk drawers, though she knew they were too small to hold the mask. She searched the closet, crawling behind the winter coats. She opened three boxes her mother had stored under the desk. And when she was done, she knew that the full-sized mask was not in the room.

Could it be anywhere else in the house? No. To preserve the mask, Mom would need tools and chemicals like those in her workroom. If the mask wasn't here, it wasn't in the house. And that meant, if Mom really had taken it, it must be down at the store.

Laney came out of the workroom. She was thinking so hard she didn't even see Rosemary watching her from the kitchen door. She was remembering how, after being gone so long in rubber boots that day, Mom had driven off in the car somewhere. Had she been taking the large mask down to the store?

And if that was where it was, Laney thought despairingly, what could she do about it?

The next day was Tuesday, Mrs. McIntyre's buying day. She was finishing her coffee when Laney came in for breakfast. "Rosemary tells me you were in my workroom again yesterday," she said at once, without even a greeting. "What were you doing there?"

Nervously, Laney licked her lips. "My good mittens were in the closet in there." It wasn't exactly a lie, she thought defensively.

Clearly her mother didn't believe her. "This must be the fourth time this week you've been in the workroom. That's more than you usually do in a year. What's the big attraction?"

"I wasn't doing anything wrong."

"It's that little mask, isn't it? You've been mooning after it ever since you gave it to me."

"I didn't give it to you," Laney said, but under her breath.

"What was that?"

"Nothing."

Her mother frowned. "I can't understand what you see in the ugly little thing. Every time I look at it I like it less." Her clever fingers played delicately with her spoon. "You didn't tell your father about it, did you?"

"I promised I wouldn't."

"That's not what I asked."

"I didn't tell him." Wearily.

Mrs. McIntyre's hand closed, briefly, on hers. Her hand felt cold and clammy. "You do keep your promises, Laney. I should have known you wouldn't say anything."

Impulsively Laney said, "Mom, I did some reading about false face masks. Did you know that they're—well, that some people think they're dangerous?"

"And some people think eating bacon and eggs is dangerous."

There was a tightness in her voice, an audible No Trespassing sign. But Laney couldn't just drop it. If Mom did have the large mask, she had to be warned. Doggedly she said, "Dangerous to the people who own the masks, I mean. To the people who might try to—well, to use them. I mean, suppose somebody found a mask somewhere and took it home and then wished for something, something bad—"

She stumbled to a halt, the look in her mother's eyes so daunting she couldn't continue.

"Let me get this straight," Mrs. McIntyre said. "Are we talking about *you*, Laney? You found the miniature mask and took it home, and now—"

"Not me." Not just me, Laney amended silently.

"Then what are you getting at?" Her eyes were iceberg-pale. She knew what Laney was saying, all right. Laney was certain of it.

"Nothing," Laney said, pushing her chair back. "Just some dumb stuff in a book. Stuff about the masks liking power and making their owners want it, too." Her fingers were tight on the edge of the table. She had to get away. "It was—I was just talking, I guess."

Her mother looked at her watch. "I'm going to miss my train if I don't watch out." She was on her feet in one smooth motion. "Leftovers for supper," she said. "And maybe some more of those nice new potatoes? Tell Rosemary, will you?"

And with a quick, efficient kiss on Laney's cheek, she was gone.

After school, Tom saw Laney hurrying to the bus stop. He followed her, not quite sure why. The bus pulled up then, and she boarded. Her face was set, her eyes determined. While she pushed her way down the crowded aisle, Tom boarded the bus, too. Mickey Spillane, he accused himself scornfully. But there was something about her face. . . .

Carefully he took up a position near the front door. He could just see her, holding onto the pole by the door at the back. She hadn't noticed him. Even if she did, he reassured himself, she wouldn't guess what he was doing. Anybody could go downtown.

At the corner of Dundas and Richmond she got out, leaving just time for Tom to exit the front door after her. In the surge of people boarding the bus he almost lost her. He saw her a few minutes later, though, across the street and heading down Dundas. Keeping pace with her, he stayed on his side of the street, too far away to see her expression. She walked quickly, her shoulders back. She seemed to know exactly where she was going.

At a store called Bronwyn's she stopped walking and looked through the barred glass door. Then, despite the big Closed sign, she knocked on the door. She knocked for a long time. Her back was to the street, and Tom took his chance and slipped across, stepping back into the recessed doorway of the jewelry store beside Bronwyn's. He could hear Laney knocking. He also heard when the door opened to her.

"Yes?" a man's voice said.

"I'm from Riverview High School," he heard Laney's voice say rapidly. "The school newspaper sent me to do an article on Bronwyn's. We think it's sad it's closing after all these years. I wonder if—"

"Well?"

"If, well, if maybe you could tell me—uh, us—why Bronwyn's didn't just change ownership, rather than close."

"You'd have to ask Mr. Bronwyn that," the man said. "And he isn't here."

"Is he at home?"

"No."

"Then—" determinedly "—where is he?"

"He's in the hospital."

"The hospital!" She sounded shocked and afraid.

The man's voice grew kinder. "It's not as bad as it sounds. He's just having a rest. He's run this place pretty much on his own, you know. There's a fair amount of stress associated with that, and he's getting on. His nerves—" Pause. Tom imagined a shrug.

"But if he just needs a rest—"

"A long rest," the man said. "And keeping the store going without him is impossible. If he had authorized selling it—but he won't. So there you are. But please don't publish it in your newspaper."

"I—all right." She sounded dazed, Tom thought. What was the matter with her? And there was no school newspaper that he knew of. "How long—" she began with difficulty "—how long has Mr. Bronwyn been—resting?"

"He was admitted to the hospital on Friday. Funny, I saw him the day before, and he seemed—"

"Fine? He seemed fine?"

The man's voice changed. "Listen, I'm a friend of his, and I really don't think this is the right time to do an article on him. Will you take my advice, and leave it alone?"

"All right." Tom had to strain to hear her. "All right, I won't write anything. Thanks for your help."

Tom turned his back quickly. He heard Laney walk

by, but slowly now, almost dragging her feet. After a moment he came out of hiding. She was only a short way ahead, her shoulders hunched forward, her hands in her pockets. Tom followed her to a bus stop on Richmond, where she stood in line for another bus. This was getting expensive, he thought, feeling to see if he had bus fare. A Richmond bus pulled up, and Laney got on board. The tense, closed look was back on her face. Tom climbed on the bus, too.

They got off in the posh shopping area of Richmond Row. Tom saw her heading toward a shop called Heritage Lane. He knew that that was her mother's store. So this trip had been perfectly innocent, and he'd wasted the bus fare. But he didn't know what else to do, so he kept on following her.

Laney never turned around. When she entered the store, he looked in through the window. There were only two people inside, besides the male clerk at the desk and Laney. She was saying something to the clerk, who nodded, looking bored. Then she disappeared behind a nearby curtain.

Going to see her mom, obviously, Tom thought, by now ready to give up the whole thing. Still, he had come this far, and Mickey Spillane wouldn't just go tamely home. He gave a mental shrug. There was an alley between Heritage Lane and the store next door. Without expecting anything, he followed it to its end.

A barred window and a metal door with a lock but no handle were the only openings in the bare brick facade at the back of the store. He went to the window. The bars didn't obstruct his view of the room inside, but it was a dull day, and the room unlit. Dimly he could see shelves and benches and bottles, a bare table in the center of the room, a large green-shaded light over it. This must be some kind of workroom. Nobody was in it now, though. Tom was just turning away when a door on the other side of the table opened, and the light was turned on. In its harsh glare he saw Laney.

She looked very nervous. Casting a furtive look over her shoulder, she slipped inside, shutting the door behind her. He watched, fascinated, as she began to search the room. One shelf after another, behind chairs with the stuffing coming out of them, under scratched desks, inside the carved doors of an old commode. She did it all very quickly. At last she came to a box-shaped object on an especially wide shelf. It was covered with linen, hiding what was beneath. She paused, her face uncertain. Then her hand went out to grasp a corner of the cloth. She gave it a yank, and the cloth came off. And under the cloth, trapped in a tank full of liquid, was the false face god.

Tom's breath caught. Blood pounded in his head, washing his vision in a sea of red. *Gaguwara!* Contained like *that*. It was obscene.

The blind eyes were on Laney, the appalling black and red gaze searing her. Hatred. Contempt. Hatred again. She clutched her throat, falling back; but the protruding eyes followed her even as she retreated. Tom's heart hammered, knowing what was happening, helpless to stop it. Laney knew it, too. Her hand went up, imploringly. Then she retched, a single dry heave.

Hatred. Hatred. Her eyes streamed with the pain of it. Unloved and stupid, nobody's friend. What good was she to anybody? What good was she even to herself?

She heaved again, and still nothing came up. Her skin was almost translucent. Her eyes shifted, guilty and desperate, blind to everything but what she was seeing in herself. She didn't see Tom, but he saw her. He read those horrified green eyes, and what he read there appalled him. The mask was making her hate herself. And that wasn't right. God or no god, Indian or white, what was happening here was wrong.

Gaguwara! his mind cried out. *Let her alone!*

The sightless gaze turned to him, a shattering blast of nausea and hate. He jerked his head away, briefly seeing Laney's hand go forward. The cloth was in it. *Throw it!* he urged her. *Cover that tank!* In that short moment of freedom, Laney obeyed. It was like turning out a light.

Laney put her face in her hands. Tom blinked rapidly. The tank might have been an ordinary aquarium. Covered, it had no power at all.

For now, it was over. Tom's mind echoed the words again and again. He stumbled down the alley, getting away. It was over.

Until the next time.

LANEY WAS IN BED, PILED HIGH WITH BLANKETS. HAMBONE was beside her, but still she couldn't stop shivering. Hatred. Contempt. Seeing herself like that. She held tight to Hambone, her lifeline.

She did have friends! Sure, she didn't have anyone like Susan anymore, but there was still Jennifer, in French class, and— And she wasn't dumb! Only at math and phys ed, and nobody could be good at everything. She was third from the top in science, wasn't she?

And she wasn't unloved; she wasn't!

She hugged Hambone so tightly he whined. The clock ticked. Outside, it was already getting dark.

Had she managed to get out of the store without anyone noticing how upset she was? She tried to remember. She knew she'd practically fallen coming into the showroom. She'd pretended to trip on the rug, but had that clerk of Mom's believed it? He must have wondered why she'd spent so long in the bathroom, the only excuse for going back there that she'd been able to invent. If he was suspicious, if he told Mom that Laney had been alone in the workroom area for that long a time . . .

Rosemary's radio blared out suddenly. It was so loud Laney could make out the lyrics even through two closed doors. She pounded furiously on the wall. After a moment, the volume was turned down. It was a victory, but it didn't make her feel even the slightest bit better.

Tom was sprawled on his bed, watching the shadows grow. He didn't know what to do. All his plans had centered on finding the large mask. He'd had only a vague idea of what to do once he had found it, something like persuading the owner to give or sell it to them and then, with Laney, burying the two masks in the bog where they belonged. But everything was changed now. Mrs. McIntyre knew too much about the value of masks like that to sell it for any amount two kids could afford. She might—his knuckles whitened at the possibility—she might not even want to sell it at all.

Briefly he thought of trying to steal the mask away from her, but the idea gave him the shudders. Steal *that mask* from a locked store with barred windows, when neither Laney nor he could bear to look at the thing, let alone touch it? Anyway, stealing the mask wouldn't make it theirs. It would still belong to Mrs.

McIntyre, because she was the one who had taken it from the bog. The death of the man who had owned it had made the mask free for the claiming, but once she had taken it, it belonged to her. It would belong to her till she died or gave it away freely. And any woman who could so calmly put *Gaguwara* in that tank wouldn't be the type to give anything valuable to anybody.

He hugged the pillow to his chest, his fingers digging deep. Until now he had thought everything might be put right, that the damage done by himself and Laney might be completely undone. What an idiot he had been! White people owning the masks. Two separate owners. The danger of it hammered at him. Could he be overdramatizing things? He wanted to believe it. But he had seen that mask. He knew what it was. He closed his eyes, remembering, imagining. Power flowing from mask to owner and owner to mask, feeding on each other, growing. And nothing to stop it, only the owner's decency, her—soul. If her soul could stand up to it. If it was the kind of soul that would even want to. The small mask protecting the wrong person and unable to restrain the large. The large mask free to work on its owner's desires and resentments, and to give her power to do something about them. It made him sick, physically sick.

Did Mrs. McIntyre know yet what she had, covered

up in her workroom? Did she really imagine she was going to be able to sell it?

If she did, maybe there was still time.

But he had never seen such hatred as the mask had aimed at Laney today. Was it because Laney owned the minimask, and the large mask was still afraid of its control? Or was it something more personal than that?

Tom covered his head with the pillow. But nothing could stop him from remembering Laney's face staring down at the mask in that harsh green light, caught like a fish in a whirlpool. The small mask ought to have protected her! It ought to have helped its rightful owner when the large mask attacked her! That was part of its function, to help its owner fight the dangers of the large mask. So why hadn't it done anything?

Or maybe it had. Maybe it had been the small mask that had given Laney the strength and speed to fling that cloth, before it was too late. Maybe that had been all the small mask could do, from a distance, and in someone else's actual keeping.

Maybe, maybe, maybe! When was he going to stop guessing and figure out what to do?

He threw the pillow across the room. It hit the hockey stick in the corner, sending it clattering to the floor. From the tree outside his window, a startled bird squawked, then took itself off into darkness. Tom chewed at his lip, thinking and thinking. What to do? What? He got to his feet, then paced the floor. His head ached with thinking. Why did everything have to be up to him? It had been Laney who had started all this, by digging in the bog in the first place. Why shouldn't he just let her pay the consequences?

But her face haunted him. He saw her walking alone, always alone, in the halls at school. He saw her defending the big, yellow dog from the threat of Animal Control. He saw her offering to walk home with him that day, afraid of his rejection, her eyes showing that she thought of him as a boy, not an Indian. He saw her talking to him at school, not caring or even noticing that other people were watching.

She wasn't like the others. She didn't deserve what was happening to her.

He went over to the window, then stared out into the dark. He let himself consider something that would have shocked him, even just a week ago. Suppose he called the Indian Museum staff? They had handled masks before. And they had been sensitive enough to remove the real one from display, when the Indians had asked. What if he told them Mrs. McIntyre was selling the large mask illegally?

They'd take it away from her, he knew. It would still be rightfully hers, but at least that would be the museum's problem, not his. He rubbed his forehead.

Maybe, for them, it wouldn't even be a problem. Maybe all that classifying and preserving and studying and analyzing would take enough of the magic out of the mask so that it would be safer.

Another Indian power destroyed by the white man. No, he couldn't do it. He wouldn't!

There wasn't a single right thing to do. Or maybe there was, and he was just the wrong person to figure it out. This was an Indian problem. Maybe he simply wasn't Indian enough to solve it.

He needed help. He needed people who knew the false face masks and how to appease the god with the twisted face. He needed the Reserve. He got to his feet and went to find his mother.

She was in the kitchen, humming to herself as she cut up potatoes.

"Mom," he said, "I want to go back to the Reserve."

She stopped humming. The knuckles whitened on the hand that was holding the knife. She put the other behind her. "We've been through this and through this," she said. "You promised me you'd try to adjust to London. You've only been here three months. And already you want to go back."

"Not to—" he began, then stopped. "I meant a visit. I need to talk to people."

Her eyes were full of hurt. He knew what she was thinking. But she didn't say it. "When?" she asked.

"Now. This weekend. As soon as I can."

She was silent for a long time. Then, tiredly, she said, "I'll drive you."

"Thanks," he said gruffly. He walked out of the room. He had to. If he had let himself stay, he would have told her everything.

EVEN AT EIGHT ON A SATURDAY MORNING, HIGHWAY 401 was jammed with cars and trucks. A brand new Mercedes, its bumper sticker reading "Born to shop"; a horse trailer, a tail hanging out the back; a rusty Plymouth full of teenagers; a convoy of seven Canadian Tire tractor trailers. The only thing most of them had in common was where they were going: Toronto, their Mecca.

Toronto wasn't Tom's Mecca. He had never been there, but he'd formed some ideas about it. Most of the tourists who came to the Reserve were from there. "What, no Visa or MasterCard?" they'd exclaim at Min's or any of the other crafts stores that dotted Ohsweken. "No checks, either? What do you expect us to pay with?"

And invariably, they laughed to see a Chinese restaurant on the Chiefswood Road.

Tom was making himself think about Toronto, as he'd made himself think about the painting he was going to do in art class next week and what he was going to buy for his mother's birthday in November. For the first time in his life, he didn't want to think about the Reserve. His mother's disapproval about this trip was only part of the reason. The rest was fear. He didn't let himself wonder why he was afraid.

After they took the 403 turnoff, the traffic thinned out. Here the country looked familiar. The rolling land, the cornfields, the tobacco kilns, the wooded valley of the Grand River—all of these were home. The big, green water tower of Brantford came into view, proclaiming itself "The Telephone City" although it was Joseph Brant it had been named for, Joseph Brant, the Indian chief. Tom's heart was thudding. Highway 54, then, winding its way along the banks of the Grand. The churchlike Onondaga Municipal building, with its bear flag surmounted by a Canadian maple leaf. And finally, finally, the signpost he'd been watching for: OHSWEKEN, 3KM.

They turned, following the Chiefswood Road over the new bridge. Six Nations Reserve, a sign said; population 7000. Except for that sign, they might have been anywhere in rural Ontario. The road was paved, the houses moderately prosperous. There were cars in every driveway. There were telephone poles and hydro wires, fire hydrants, television antennas. Tom had never noticed any of these things before. They had been here, but he had taken them for granted. Now he noticed them. Now he was almost listing them in his mind.

Why? The Community Health Centre, the Iroquois Lodge, the Alcohol and Drug Centre, all new in the last ten years; the shopping plaza with its launderette and video rental; the park with its cannons and public library. Hardly anyone outside. He couldn't stop noticing things. He tried and tried, but he couldn't.

"Where to?" his mother asked. Once, automatically, she would have turned left at the Fourth Line, heading for the Onondaga Road, and home.

"I want to go to our house," Tom said defiantly.

"It belongs to somebody else now, or have you forgotten?"

"I just want to look at it."

Home. The four-room cottage with its brand-new roof and bright blue siding and the rotting back porch for which Mom had been saving her writing money to fix. The garden whose vegetables Mrs. Walsh had served, day in and day out, every summer. The wilderness of meadow flowers—white boneset spiking out amid the daisies, the dotting purple of wild asters, the yellow blankets of goldenrod. Land cleared but not farmed, and only the Indian Act to explain why.

In silence, Mrs. Walsh turned left, following the Fourth Line. The split-level houses that lined its paved surface might have comfortably sat on Riverside Drive. At Stoneridge Church, Mrs. Walsh slowed, then kept on. Normally they would have turned here, heading left up Onondaga Road for Silversmith Corners. But not today. Tom's hands clenched and unclenched. He knew what this meant. They were going to take Cayuga Road, the road with the cemetery.

She stopped when they got there, undoing her seat belt. "Are you coming?"

He looked the other way. He had never gone to his father's grave, not after the first time. After a moment his mother left him. Steadily, steadily, Tom looked away. Was that a hawk on that branch over there? It rose into the sky. Just a crow, after all. A car went by, stirring up so much dust he couldn't see anyone inside. Half an hour on the Reserve, and the only people he'd seen were blurs from a car window.

Five minutes away was the Fifth Line. He let himself think about that, about the gravel road with its immobile trailers and its houses with their unpainted particle-board siding; about the two longhouses located on it; about his own house, halfway between the two. But even the Fifth Line was dangerous to think about. Because it had been on that road, five months ago, that a car driven by a drunk had barreled into his father and killed him.

Tom had not cried. Not once, in five months, had he cried.

After a long time, Mrs. Walsh came back to the car. She slid behind the wheel but didn't turn on the motor. "There was a whole family of rabbits out there," she said. "One of them was standing up on its back legs on your father's stone, sniffing at the wind and keeping an eye out for danger. I saw meerkats do that once, in a zoo. They even warn each other about airplanes, did you know? The whole lot'll go diving for cover, and then way, way up in the sky, a plane'll go by. It doesn't even know about the meerkats trembling and hiding in their little secret spots."

Tom was silent. After a moment, his mother turned on the engine. "Time to go home," she said, her voice ironic and deep.

When they got there, there was a baby playing in the front yard and two filthy older children and a big dog that ran to the road and silently bared its teeth at them. The new, blue siding of the house was spattered with mud. At the side of the house the vegetable garden was a mass of dying weeds. The old dead elm that George Walsh had refused to cut down was gone.

Mrs. Walsh slowed, then looked questioningly at Tom. He couldn't say anything. He just shook his head. She stepped on the accelerator again, and they went on.

"Onondaga Longhouse?" he asked after a minute.

His mother shrugged. "It's your party." She took the turn onto Onondaga Road.

It was almost certainly too late in October for the Harvest Festival. On Saturday, this early in the morning, there might not even be a Faith Keeper there. But it was the only place Tom could think of where he might get in touch with someone in the False Face Society.

Mrs. Walsh's old Dodge left the crossroads behind, and woodland and meadow closed in on either side. After a few minutes they passed a Hansel-and-Gretel path on the right. Then, in a clearing to the left, the green roof and twin chimneys of Onondaga Longhouse came into view. Mrs. Walsh pulled the car up into the graveled space in front of the rusting iron gate that separated the longhouse from the road. She turned off the engine. Neither of them said a word. They only looked.

It wasn't what the tourists expected, when they came. It was an ordinary-looking house and not even very long. Its white clapboard was badly in need of paint. The front stoop was deeply creviced. The well in the graveled yard had long been capped. There were hydro wires. There was a sign declaring that this was Onondaga Longhouse, and under it was posted an announcement for a meeting that had taken place six months before. The last time Tom had been here, the announcement had been only three months out of date. The two outbuildings were as much shacks as ever. Only their windows were brand-new, still with the manufacturer's stickers on them. But those windows were always either broken or brand-new. It was the way of things, on the Reserve.

Tom stared straight in front of him, observing everything, unable to say a word. Nothing had changed here, nothing at all. But he wasn't seeing it the same way. He was looking at it as a stranger would. Shaken, he looked away.

"Well?" his mother asked challengingly.

Tom made himself reach for the door. "I might be a while."

"I'll wait in the car. That's what you want, isn't it?"

"You could go and get some coffee."

"Thanks," his mother said dryly. "Considerate of you."

"It's not what you think," Tom said, fast and desperate. "I'm not just trying to get rid of you."

"Aren't you? Well, never mind. I'll be back in a couple of hours. You go and do your thing. But Tom—"

"Yes?"

She sighed. "Nothing. Just go."

The door was locked, so he sat on the front stoop. It was very quiet. In the distance he could hear a dog barking, and somewhere crows were squawking. An isolated car started up, sounding far away and not very real. Later there came the sound of wheels on gravel, a bicycle ridden toward the longhouse. Tom was down at the road before it came into view. He knew the boy riding it, Peter Logan, a kid his own age. They'd been in the same class at school, although they'd never been friends.

"Hey, Pete," Tom said.

The bicycle skidded to a stop. "Heya, Tom. Whatcha doing here? Thought you'd moved to Toronto."

"London." He grimaced, but the expected sympathy didn't come.

"You'd fit right in there, I'd'a thought."

"What's that supposed to mean?"

Peter shrugged, still sitting on the saddle. "If you can't figger it out—" He put his feet back on the pedals. "Have a nice visit," he said very politely, and rode off.

Ten minutes later, an old man came. He was another Logan, but no relation to Peter. Tom had seen him often at the longhouse, and last midwinter he had been one of the two Doorkeepers, the one that made sure no one left the longhouse without participating in the Round Dance. Tom remembered seeing him take off his false face when it was over, his lined brown face glistening with sweat and tiredness.

The old man closed the gate behind him, then headed for the cookhouse with a bag in his hand. He didn't appear to see the boy hesitating on the longhouse's front stoop. Nervously, Tom called after him. "Mr. Logan. Mr. Logan!" But if the man heard, he made no sign. Slowly and steadily, he made for the cookhouse.

Tom didn't wait. He ran after the old man, and caught him just as he reached the cookhouse door. "Mr. Logan," he said breathlessly. "You won't remember me, but I'm—"

Slowly the man turned. His eyes were milky with cataracts. "You're the white woman's son," he said, slow and uninterested.

Tom stepped back. "I—I'm George Walsh's son, too."

"George Walsh. Ahh." He turned away.

Tom plucked at his sleeve. "Mr. Logan. Please. I—I have to talk to you. It's about a *face*."

"What have you to do with *faces*? What has any white person to do with them?"

There was a pain in Tom's stomach, sharp and achy as a sickness. White person. Was that what they thought about him? Was that what they had always thought? "I'm not white," he whispered.

"People are what they are," the old man said distantly.

There was no use protesting. And this man might be the only one who could help him. "I found a *face* in a bog," he said rapidly. "It was an old one. There was a miniature with it. Now they belong to two separate people. They're both—both the people are—white."

"That is dangerous," Mr. Logan said. He turned away again.

"Wait," Tom pleaded. "Isn't there anything—can't you do something? The Society of Faces, I mean?"

"It is nothing to do with us."

"These masks aren't like the stuff they sell at Min's," Tom said urgently. "They're the real thing. And white people own them."

"White people own everything."

"You could take them back. It's against the law for them to—"

"White man's laws!"

"You don't want them," Tom said, with sudden understanding. "That's it, isn't it? You just don't want them."

Mr. Logan shrugged. "We have our own *faces*."

"But these are real," Tom repeated, feeling as if he were speaking a foreign language. "They're old. They're Iroquois heritage. How can you just let them go? Even if there isn't a museum here—"

"Are we white men, to seek the dead in museums?"

"But the two people who've got those masks don't understand what they have. Those masks will destroy them!"

"Whites have never understood what they have. They had forests, and they made cities. They had clear streams, and they made cesspools. The whites take, and so shall they receive."

"But they're not just whites! They're people, too!"

Silence. Shocked, on both sides.

"And one of them," Tom added slowly, discovering it for the first time, "is my friend."

"Then it is you who must help them, not we." And he pushed open the cookhouse door and went inside.

Tom went away from the longhouse. The Reserve was a foreign place, and he was a foreigner in it. He walked and walked and felt no belonging. Go home, he thought. But there was no home. There was only London and here.

When he became aware of his surroundings again, he was on the Cayuga Road in front of the cemetery. Slowly, he made his way inside. The stone was set into the earth, a simple slab. *George Walsh,* it said, *age 35.* There were fresh flowers on it, wildflowers, the kind his mother liked.

For a long time Tom stared down at the grave. An Indian, he thought, a pure-bred Iroquois. For fourteen years Tom had tried to be as Indian as he was. Fourteen years, Tom thought, and he himself had never seen, never once understood. The Indian who had loved a white woman had not belonged on this Reserve. He had not belonged on any Reserve. He had seen people as people, regardless of the color of their skin. He belonged to a world that didn't yet exist.

And Tom, who had hardly ever looked even at his own mother without seeing her whiteness, put his face in his hands, and he cried.

SUNDAY MORNING AGAIN. RAIN POURED DOWN, ENDLESS as tears. Laney stared into her corn flakes. Her mother was reading the *Star,* as intent as if she were alone. It was always like that now, ever since Laney had tried to warn her about the mask. Now and then Mom suggested a warmer coat or what to have for dinner, and she was always pleasant whenever Laney spoke, but she never really talked to her, and she always broke off the attempts Laney made. She was as polite to Laney as if she were a stranger.

Laney stirred her cereal, uncaring that it had already turned to mush. Five days had passed since she had discovered that her mother did have the mask. Five nights of dreams that made her wake with her face buried in her pillow, choking down screams. And what had she done about it? Nothing.

But what could she have done? Tell Dad about the masks, when she'd made a solemn oath not to? Could she dare risk it when it might send Mom to jail? Tell the museum? That would be just as bad. Tom? He'd probably just say they had to get the big mask back. And even if she could have faced going back into Mom's workroom at the store again, the thought of taking that mask into her own possession, or letting Tom take it, made her skin crawl. Nobody should have that mask. Nobody.

There was something she could have done if she had been braver. She had thought of it late Thursday night, when the dreams had left her wide-eyed and trembling in the dark. What she could have done, what she should have done on Tuesday, was to dump the mask out of its preserving bath and leave it to rot. But the mask had been too strong for her. It would be too strong again. Anyway, it was too late now. Today Mom would be taking the masks out of their preserving solution for their final drying. From now on there would be no question of their rotting. They would be preserved forever.

That mask, that terror, existing forever.

Rosemary yawned her way into the room. "Wouldn't you just know it'd be raining? Dad'll take me to the boring old art gallery—you just watch!"

"You may wish he had," Alicia McIntyre said. "There's going to be a public meeting this afternoon about that bog development. And you know your father."

Rosemary groaned. "I think I'll get sick. Don't you think I look sick? God, aren't Sundays awful?"

For once Laney totally agreed with her. Two Sundays

ago she had found the mask. Last Sunday had been that thing with Hambone and her mother. Today . . . What would happen today?

By ten o'clock the rain had drizzled away to a kind of Scottish mist, and Laney decided to take Hambone for a walk. She didn't want to be around when her father arrived to pick up Rosemary. The temptation to tell him about the masks might prove too much for her.

She went down by the river. They walked for hours, Hambone silent and watchful, tuned in to Laney's mood. Laney hardly noticed him. She was trying to be sensible, trying to convince herself that nothing terrible was actually going on. So much of what had happened was based on interpretation, on her own imagination, on Tom's. She needed facts, not superstitions mentioned in a book or handed to her by a boy who had grown up on Indian legends.

What were the facts? What events—not feelings, but actual happenings—had taken place since those masks had come to light?

She stopped walking and stared at the river, clearing her mind. A list, she would make a list. When it was written down, she would know. She had a notebook and a pencil in her pocket. She got them out.

One. Rosemary had gotten sick after Laney ill-wished her. That looked silly, written down. Laney read it, then scribbled something else. She wrote that the doctor had said it was food poisoning, and that Rosemary herself had said her burger had tasted funny. The first sentence looked even sillier now.

Two. Mom had hit Hambone. She'd never done that before, never. But sometimes people do do things they've never done before. And she *had* been really angry.

Three. Mom had ill-wished Hambone, and he'd gotten sick, just like Rosemary. But he had been eating garbage. Carefully, she wrote that down, followed by a large question mark.

Four. Laney had asked the little mask to heal Hambone, and he'd stopped being sick right away. But what if he'd been going to get better just then anyway, and her visit to the mask had been just good timing?

Five. Bronwyn's had closed its doors forever, just as Mom had always wanted. And why? Because Mr. Bronwyn had had some kind of sudden mental breakdown starting almost as soon as Mom had gotten the large mask. And masks did have the power to make people ill, mentally as well as physically. She erased that part. That wasn't a fact. That was just something some people believed.

Six. Mom had kept the large mask a secret. And why wouldn't she, if she was already worried about Laney telling Dad she had the small one?

Seven. Mom was beginning to hate the small mask. She'd said so. She hadn't disliked it at first, before she found the big one. If the big mask really did hate the small one, and if Mom really was getting possessed by the . . .

Laney stopped herself. Objects didn't hate each other, not in real life. Even less did people get possessed by things. Obsessed, maybe. But possessed, ruled, taken over by something that wasn't even alive, no way. That part wasn't fact; it was superstition.

There wasn't anything else. Seven facts, that was all, and every one of those facts could be explained away. And against them, nothing but feelings. The large mask's malice, intangible but staggering. The suffocating nightmares that had followed her discovery of it. The ambivalence she felt when she looked at the small mask, loving it but afraid of it, afraid because she kept thinking it was trying to protect her and she didn't want to need its protection, afraid because she imagined it offered her power. And, finally, the tension in the McIntyre house. The constant scorn and bickering and unpleasantness. The hatred. Laney shook her head in denial, but the thought couldn't be pushed away. Hatred in her own house. Hatred against her.

Events set in motion. Events that had to be played out.

Feelings couldn't matter as much as facts; they couldn't. Laney looked at the pages she'd written on, then tore them to pieces. She wound Hambone's leash tightly around her palm and began to run. She ran and ran, but when she stopped, panting and exhausted, the fear was still there. All the logic in the world couldn't change that.

She was afraid to go home.

"Yes, Joe, you heard me. No full-sized mask. I've decided not to sell it. . . . Well, I'm sorry, but we never signed anything, did we? Look, it won't make any difference how much you offer. If you must know, I happen to want it for myself. . . . Yes, the minimask is still for sale." Exasperated: "I know they'd bring me more as a pair! But will you get it into your head, the full-sized mask is out of it. If you don't want the minimask, let me know. I won't have any trouble finding someone who does."

Mrs. McIntyre slammed down the receiver. Her impatient footsteps sounded, coming toward the living room door. Laney fled up the hall to her own room, closing the door just in time. She leaned against it, breathing hard. She hadn't intended to listen in. But how could she pass by without listening when her mother had been talking about the mask?

Her mother, who didn't care about owning old things, only about selling them. Her mother, who'd said the minimask alone would go for ten thousand dollars at least. Her mother, now saying that it didn't matter how much anyone offered for the large one, because she wanted it for herself.

Fact number eight, Laney thought dazedly.

Outside, a car started up. Laney went to her window. In the growing dark, with the mist hanging in the air, the headlights of Mrs. McIntyre's car seemed fuzzy and unreal. Where was Mom going, at six o'clock on a Sunday night, with the roast beef done and waiting? Why hadn't she said anything to Laney? And why wasn't Rosemary home?

Alone, Laney thought. Only Hambone and the mini-mask down the hall to keep her company. She opened the door, then almost ran to the living room. She found the telephone book, but her hands were shaking and it was hard to find the right page. Walsh, she thought feverishly. Riverside Drive. Here it was. She picked up the phone, and she dialed.

A boy's voice answered. "Tom?" she asked.

He knew who it was. "Yes, it's me," he answered. There was a long pause. "What's wrong?" he asked, sudden and sharp.

"I—I've got something to tell you. It's about that mask."

"The big one?"

Behind her, the front door opened. "Well, good night," Rosemary's voice said, not troubling to hide her boredom.

"Good night," said Dr. McIntyre, a little dryly.

"Laney?" Tom said. "Are you there?"

"Yes, yes, I'm here. Listen, Rosemary's home. Can I talk to you tomorrow?"

"When?"

"Lunch?"

"Okay. See you then."

"Okay. And Tom—"

"Yeah?"

"Thanks."

Laney put the phone down and turned to see Rosemary. Her sister was in a bad mood. "Don't you ever get tired of chasing that kid?" she sneered. "But I guess Tom Walsh is the best someone like you can do."

She swirled off into the kitchen. Laney's relief evaporated, and anger took its place. Who did Rosemary think she was? Sniping at Tom, digging at her, acting as if they'd both crawled out from under rocks. As if Laney were nothing, a zero, a dirty old doormat. She wasn't! Just because Rosemary was pretty and clever and people liked her, just because Mom was always on her side . . . Rage clotted in Laney's heart, a cold, hard knot of hate.

Down the hall, sitting on a rack where the air could dry it evenly, something stirred. Laney felt it; she knew what it was. A little piece of wood, a soldier blindly awaiting orders. Why shouldn't Rosemary be on the receiving end for a change? Why shouldn't she find out how it felt? One word from Laney, that was all it would take. Whatever happened, it would serve Rosemary right!

Laney put her hands over her face, struggling with

that thing down the hall, with herself. The first time, she had not known she could hurt Rosemary. Her ill wish had been made on impulse only, not with any real malice. But if she did it this time—if she chose, actually chose to hurt someone with the small mask—

Time passed. Slowly, the rage left her. She put her hands down. Her muscles felt weak. She felt no pride, no sense of safety. This time, she had kept control. But another time she might not. Another time, she might give way altogether.

And this was just the small mask, she reminded herself. How much harder it must be to resist the large one!

Why did Mom want that mask? What was she going to do with it?

And what, oh what, was it going to do with them?

LANEY WAS DREAMING AGAIN. SHE WAS IN A HUT OF WOVEN branches. It was long, very long, and so thick with smoke that she couldn't see the end. Tiered platforms lined it on either side. People sat there, but she wasn't one of them. A single person stood on a bench, singing. The singer's voice was muffled, lost in the vastness of that place. Smoke wreathed his body. His upraised hand flickered red in the firelight.

Shouts. Someone, something, entered the east doorway. It wore a corn-braided mask: a husk face, long-nosed, funny and terrible. There it was, now, crabbing along four-legged, heading for the fire. Tobacco and wood smokes blended, while the singer invoked:

Partake of this sacred tobacco, you Husk Faces. You, too, have done your duty.

Now, wooden faces, rough, deformed, figures crippled below the waist, hunchbacked. Creeping in, sticks in hand, rattling.

And you, too, whose faces are against the trees in the forests, whom we call the Society of Faces, you also receive tobacco.

Dancing. Hot ashes blowing, as the singer's voice shrilled its final summons: *O mighty Shagodyoweh, whose other name is Gaguwara, you who live at the rim of the earth, you who travel everywhere caring for the people, enter now and partake of the sacred tobacco.*

Now the west door. She could not see it at first, but still she knew. It was the god of the world's rim. It was the Doctor and the Destroyer. And it was wearing the face from the bog.

The Doorkeeper barred the way after it. No one now could enter or leave. A new song rose, strange and unclear. Smoke wreathed upward, dizzying. A bent knee jerked into view, then was gone. Stones rattled in turtle shells. Ashes passed through Laney, burning her soul.

And now the Round Dance. Foot lifted, heel bumped, one ahead of the other, continual. One Doorkeeper preventing escape. Another directing the dance. Songs, continual, ever-changing. Foot up, bump, foot up, bump. Endless. Someone trying to escape. The others fighting him. Dance. Dance. Everyone must dance. Dance!

Laney danced. They did not see her. She danced.

Gaguwara's hands thrust into the flames, unburnt; wooden lips blew ashes into the face of illness. Healing. Tobacco the payment, corn mush, kettles of bear fat, the worship of the people. It was over.

For one, it was over forever. That one lay crooked and inert on the longhouse floor. On his head was the face of a god. And off in the corner under a bench, a miniature mask reposed, lost from the dance, escaping.

Mine, Laney thought; and in her dream, like an upraised wail, *Will it abandon me, too?*

Monday broke windless and clear, but even at noon it was too cold to eat outside. Laney and Tom met in the cafeteria, arriving late enough to be able to find a table to themselves. Rosemary was still there, though, sitting with Web and a couple of other kids. She said something when she saw Laney with Tom, and a loud laugh went up. Laney didn't let herself look.

"Some people have sisters," Tom said casually, "and some have barracudas."

"Now and then she's okay," Laney said.

"Sure." He took a bite of his sandwich. "So what were you going to tell me about that mask?"

Carefully Laney opened her brown bag, getting out a sandwich and an apple and two Oreo cookies, spreading them out before her. For a long time she just looked at them. Then she said, "I've found it. The big mask, I mean."

"I know," Tom said. "I followed you to your mom's store. I was looking through the back window when you found it."

"You saw—" Shaken, Laney broke off. She was relieved not to have to explain, but she didn't like the idea of being followed. She particularly didn't like it that Tom might have witnessed what that mask had done to her. She lifted her chin at him. "Pretty sneaky, following me."

"Pretty sneaky not to say your mom had that mask."

"I didn't know for sure she did," she protested, "not until I went to the store."

"But you guessed."

"What if it had been your mom? Wouldn't you have made sure first, before you told anybody?"

"My mom would never have stolen Indian artifacts in the first place."

Angrily she got to her feet. He caught her arm. "About that mask, Laney. It doesn't exactly love you, you know." She only looked at him. He changed tactics. "What did you go to Bronwyn's for?"

"He's gone out of business. He had a nervous breakdown. It happened in the last two weeks, since I—since Mom—" She was sitting down again, her head close to Tom's, speaking urgently, not even noticing the looks that came their way. "Don't you see, Bronwyn's was Mom's biggest competitor!"

Tom did see. He saw very well. If Laney's mother had wished Bronwyn's would close, the mask could easily have made Mr. Bronwyn too sick to keep going. But Laney was so upset, he had to try to comfort her. "Even if Bronwyn's closed because of the mask," he pointed out, "your mother might not have done it on purpose."

"I know. I didn't, when I—when Rosemary got sick. It's just that, well, Mom's so different, these days." It came out in a rush. "She got so mad at Hambone, I thought she was going to—well, anyway, he got really sick."

"Your mother used the mask against him?"

"I don't know. I don't know! He was eating garbage. He might—"

"What was that you said about Rosemary getting sick?"

"That wasn't Mom's fault," Laney said.

"Whose, then?"

Laney was grinding a cookie to crumbs against the table. "I was mad at her," she whispered. "I made a wish." She raised her eyes to Tom's. "The doctor gave her some medicine. He said it was food poisoning. And she did get better."

"Did Hambone?"

"I—I asked the little mask to—" She broke off. "He's all right."

Tom knew enough not to push it. There was plenty to think about, anyway. Willed sickness. The hatred that mask in the store had displayed for Laney. Laney trying to undo with the small one what the large one might have done to Hambone. Mask against mask. Mother against daughter. He shook his head, very disturbed.

And Mrs. McIntyre. If Hambone's illness was indeed

due to the large mask, and if Bronwyn's closing was, too—well, that would be twice that something she wished for had come true. And being an antique dealer, she must know something about the legends associated with Iroquois masks. Even if the first two occasions had been accidents, she must be beginning to figure things out by now.

And did that make things better or worse?

Laney looked up from the cookie she had annihilated. "There's more," she said heavily. "At first, Mom was going to sell both the masks. I heard her talking on the phone. But now she's not. She could get thousands and thousands of dollars for the big one, but she says she wants to keep it. She doesn't *do* that, Tom. We don't have a single antique in our whole house. Why does she want to keep *it* if she doesn't—if it isn't—?"

"What about the small one?" Tom asked. "She doesn't want to keep that, too, does she?" Not in a million years, he thought. Not if she really was trying to use the large mask. The small mask would put too many limits on it.

"No, she's selling that one." She rubbed her forehead, a desperate movement. "Tom, we've got to get her away from that big mask!"

"Even if we could, she'd still own it. She took it from the body. She'll own the mask till she dies, or until she gives it up of her own free will."

"She'll never do that."

"What about you? Could you give up yours?"

"Give up mine?" She gaped at him.

"The small mask." The idea had just come to him. "The one *you* took from the body. Could you give it up?"

Give it up. Lose its protection, leave herself open to dangers she was only now beginning to recognize. Her dream came to her again. The mask's protection gone. Its power gone, too; and the healing she could do with it; and the other things.

"What you have to do," Tom said, the plan now set firmly in his head, "is to give the little mask to your mother."

"But she already has it!"

"She has it, but she doesn't own it. You do. Don't you see, that's half the problem. The small mask's protecting you, not her, from the other one's power. Your mom hasn't got any protection from its darker side. But if you give her the little mask, things'll be back the way they ought to be. It will help control how much the large one affects her."

Laney considered this. It made a kind of sense. The only trouble was, Mom didn't like the small mask. She wouldn't accept it, even if Laney could make herself give it away. "I can't see her taking it from me, Tom. Even if she did, it wouldn't be hers for long. She's going to sell it, I told you."

"What if you give it to her without her knowing? Maybe tie it to the hair of the big mask, where it belongs?"

Tie it to the mask! Touch, actually touch, that hate-filled face! "Mom would see it," she protested, looking for excuses.

"Maybe not right away. And if the two masks are tied together for a while, maybe she won't even mind by the time she does see it. Maybe she'll have gotten enough of her senses back that she'll realize that's the way things ought to be."

"Maybe, maybe, maybe!" Explosively she echoed his own uncertainty. She wasn't sure she could bring herself to give up the small mask, but even more than that, she was afraid of the process he had described. "Tom, I don't want to go back to the store. I don't ever want to have anything to do with the big mask again!"

"Do you think I do?"

They stared at each other. But it was a plan, a chance for a way out. And it was the only one either of them could think of. Laney dropped her eyes.

"You'll have to get hold of the small mask," Tom said, making his voice businesslike. "Can you do that, without your mom finding out?"

"I guess so." Unwillingly.

Tom tried to reassure her. "Look, you will have the small mask with you. It's yours until you give it up. It'll protect you until then. Tying it to the large mask will be your way of giving it up. After that, the two masks will be too occupied with each other to worry about us." Behind his back, he crossed his fingers.

"You'd be there with me?" Laney whispered, ashamed of the relief that filled her.

"We're in this together." His voice was gruff.

Warmth crept into Laney's heart. None of this was Tom's problem. It wasn't Tom who kept wanting to—do things; it wasn't *his* mother who had turned into a stranger. He had figured out a plan that might help, and now instead of just going home and leaving her to do it, he was going to help. He was as afraid as she was of that mask, and he was still going to help. Inarticulate with gratitude, she thrust her hand across the table at him.

He was so surprised, he took it. It felt unexpectedly good. Her eyes were pretty, he thought. He had never noticed that before. The thought flustered him, and he dropped her hand. Across the room, someone tittered. Neither of them noticed. "And we'll have to get into your mother's store," he said, making himself think about the plan. "Can you get her keys?"

"She keeps a spare set in her desk. If I waited till she was asleep, I could get them. But she might find out in the morning."

"You'll have them back into her desk by then."

"You can't get keys copied that late at night." He was silent, letting her figure it out. "You mean we're going to face that thing in the middle of the night?" she asked slowly. "When? Not tonight?"

"You got any other plans?" He was proud of how

matter-of-fact he sounded. "It's better than tomorrow night, anyway."

"Why?"

"Because tomorrow's Halloween." He took aim with his lunch bag, then tossed it into the garbage can against the wall. "And I've got a feeling our own two masks are going to keep us busy enough, without having to worry about a lot of the other kind, too."

THE HOUSE WAS SILENT. THERE WERE NO LIGHTS ON ANYwhere. In her bedroom, Laney was watching the moon. Tonight it was almost full, a white ball crisscrossed by the branches of the tree outside her window. Mom's spare key case was sweaty in her fingers. Behind her, quiet but insistent, her new alarm clock ticked.

It was a few minutes past twelve-thirty. At one she would slip down the hall to her mother's workroom and get the little mask. At one-fifteen she would be on her bike, whose tires she had pumped that evening almost to bursting. By two she would be parking her bike in the little courtyard behind her mother's store.

She imagined it all, a mental rehearsal. Which roads to take, whether she would stop for traffic lights, whether to take the alley from Richmond Street to the courtyard or come at it from the back. She'd been in the courtyard lots of times, because all the store owners in that part of the block parked their cars there. But she'd never been there at night.

Ruthlessly she pictured it. It would be really dark;

the shadows of the buildings would guarantee it. Neither the streetlights nor the moon would penetrate to the big metal door that opened only inward. And behind that door, if they could really get in, would be the unlit workroom and that cloth-covered tank inside. Tom was bringing a flashlight, because turning on the overhead light might attract attention. But a flashlight wouldn't be much to hold onto in the middle of the night, everything black as tar, and that mask waiting.

Tick-tick-tick went the clock.

She hoped Tom would get there first.

Quarter to two. Richmond Street a well-lit ghost. A car went by, loud in the stillness. Tom kept riding, scrunching into his collar so that no one would see how young he was. The car disappeared. Neon lights flickered on the road. Swoosh went his bicycle wheels. Almost there now. Would Laney come? Or would she leave him waiting in the dark, with only a door between him and Gaguwara?

He had passed her house, and there had been no sign of life. He should have waited for her, he told himself. He should have made sure of her. But two kids joyriding around the streets of London after one A.M. would have been sure to attract attention.

Still, he wished she hadn't been so scared about tonight. He wished he could be more sure of her.

He could see the sign for Heritage Lane now. He slowed down a little, letting another car pass him, giving it time to get out of sight. He glanced around, making sure he had no witnesses. Then, sharply, he turned into the little alley beside the store.

Darkness lay thick on the courtyard, a muffling blanket stretching into the sky. The moon was invisible. Tom waited for a few minutes, letting his eyes get accustomed to the gloom. Then he got off his bike, leaning it against the deeper darkness of the store's back wall. He could see nothing of the metal door, but a pale shimmer told him where the window was. He was glad he'd been here once in daylight. His eyes watered with cold. It wasn't a city cold, but the dank, still cold of winter marshes. He was surrounded by buildings, but he could smell leaf mold.

Laney wasn't here yet. Well, it wasn't quite two. She still had time.

He stayed where he was, not turning on his flashlight. His heart pounded. THUD-thud-thud, THUD-thud-thud. Like the beating of a drum, he thought. THUD-thud-thud. Indian dancers moving in rhythm. Stop it, he told himself.

Somewhere, he could feel the mask.

And then he heard the spectral whir of bicycle wheels.

"Tom?"

It was a whisper, laced with panic.

He flashed on his light. "I'm here." She wheeled over to him. When she had parked her bike and was beside him, he turned off the light again. "Did you get everything?" he whispered.

"In my knapsack."

He flashed the light on again. "Let's have those keys." He held out his hand, amazingly steady.

She fumbled in her pack, then handed him the case, watching as he unzipped it. "That's the one, I think," she said, when he came to a small, modern-looking key. She was shivering, hugging her arms to her.

"We'd better get to it," Tom said. But neither of them moved. "Oh, for heaven's sake," he said irritably. He marched to the door, a little pool of light in the courtyard's vast gloom.

Laney was left alone. The darkness smothered her, full of hatred and dismay and a great, inexplicable gloating. She ran after Tom, who was shining the light back at her, wondering where she was. He had gotten the door open. A crack of absolute darkness waited behind.

"I'll go first," he whispered, when her nervous hand closed on his arm. "Just tell me which way."

"It's the—first door on the right," she got out. "Tom—"

"It's all right." He pried her hand loose. "Ready?"

She would never be ready. She nodded.

Tom shone the flashlight down the hall. He could see the door she was talking about. Something metal hung near the doorknob. He frowned. "Was there a padlock there on Tuesday?" he asked Laney.

"No-o." Her voice was jerky, shivering like the rest of her.

"Well, there's one there now."

He hurried down the hall, searching through the keycase with his fingers. But there was no key that could possibly open a padlock. He checked again. There were Yale keys and deadbolt keys and one big old-fashioned key, but the key he was looking for wasn't there. He tried a few anyway, jamming them futilely at the padlock's tiny opening. Nothing. Nothing! Suddenly he lost his temper. He gave the padlock a violent jerk, then slammed it into the door. He shook the doorknob till the hinges rattled. It was useless. He knew it was useless, and still he kept on.

"Stop it," Laney hissed. "The noise—the police—"

That halted him. Together, they held their breath, listening. Silence descended, thick as the night. No sirens, no noise at all. But behind the door, crashing on it like waves of soundless surf, something abruptly hit at them.

The Doctor, the monster, the red-clawed beast. Tom reeled. His eyes began to run, the droplets so hot they burned. His hand clutched his forehead, scrubbing at images that branded themselves behind his flesh and his bone. He fell back against the other wall of the corridor. The flashlight dropped from his hand.

Laney scrambled after it, but her hands were too

slippery to pick it up. The corridor seemed endless, the walls like white ghosts, closing in. Little bursts of terror bubbled through her lips. "Tom?" she croaked. "Tom?"

The backpack. Straps in the way, and buckles. Fingers fumbling, searching, closing at last on the miniature mask. It fitted in her palm exactly. The corridor became less narrow, the beam from the flashlight less lonely. It wasn't white anymore, but red. The corridor wasn't white either. She saw it through her eyelids, and everything seemed bathed in her own blood and pulsing with life, the way things did in summer, with the bright sun beating down. Keeping the mask in one hand, she picked up the flashlight. She shoved it into Tom's hand, wrapping his fingers around it, digging her fingernails in. When she took her hand away, little red crescents remained on his skin.

He looked down at them, stupidly. "What—?"

"Out of here! Now!"

Tom's hand hurt. She reached for it again, but he shook her off. Then he swung round on his toes, walking carefully away. Laney was close behind him. When he got outside, he pulled her through, then locked the door behind them. He stood with his back to it, looking out at a night that seemed pale compared with what they had just escaped. Laney was saying something. He didn't hear.

"Well, that's that," he said. His voice was empty, flat with the knowledge of what he had learned. Behind a locked door, and grown so powerful! How could they have imagined controlling that—thing? How could they have hoped to stop what was going to happen?

He handed her the keys. She dropped them into her pack and, after a moment, the little mask as well. It was like losing a friend. She fastened the straps hurriedly. "So, what do we do now? Tom? What are we going to do?"

"Nothing," he said. "There's not one single thing we can do."

He went over to his bike. She followed. When she had mounted, he turned off the flashlight and wheeled away. The sense of failure was so bitter he couldn't even say good-bye.

Laney was only halfway home when a patrolling police car stopped her. It was almost three in the morning, and she was weaving her bike along Queens with a weariness that looked half-drunk. She'd stopped caring that her thirteen-year-old face was perfectly visible in the streetlights. She'd stopped caring about anything.

There were two policemen in the car. "What's a kid like you doing out of bed this time of night?" the driver asked through the car window. Huge-eyed, she stared at him. "Runaway," he muttered to the other man.

"Looks more like shock, to me," the other said. "Better try to find out who she is." He got out of the car.

He took Laney's hands off the handlebars, steered her to the sidewalk, engaged the kickstand, and patted her arm kindly. "Now then, you don't need to be afraid of us. What's your name?"

"Laney," she whispered.

"Laney what? And where do you live?"

They'd call Mom; she knew it. And the small mask was in her pack, and her mother's keys. Mom would find out. Mom would know what she'd been doing.

"You're under age," the policeman said, still kind, but very firm. "You'll have to tell us. We'll find out anyway, when your parents call us."

Laney knew they were right. In the morning, with Mom making her usual Tuesday visit out of town, she might not notice that the little mask was gone, and that Laney wasn't home. But by tomorrow night the alarm would be out. Laney's only chance was to make it back before then, and in some way that the police wouldn't be involved.

How? She racked her brains. Lie about where she lived? But the police wouldn't just tamely drop her off at any old front door, giving her a chance to disappear around the back. No, they'd want to speak to whomever answered the door, and they'd want to be sure whoever it was really knew Laney. And that left only one person.

"All right," she said. "I'm Laney McIntyre. The address is 111D Airedale Street."

It was the only thing she could think of. It was her father's apartment.

For about ten seconds after Dr. McIntyre opened the door, he stood blinking at the policeman holding Laney's arm. "Laney," he said then, very quietly, "what's wrong?"

"I guess this must be your daughter," the policeman said, looking from one of them to the other and blinking at their resemblance.

"Yes."

"And she lives here?"

Dr. McIntyre hesitated for only a moment. "I have visitation rights," he said carefully.

The policeman's voice grew resigned. "A divorce case, eh? That explain why a kid like this is riding the streets at three in the morning?"

"I don't know what explains it," Dr. McIntyre said. "I intend to find out."

The policeman shrugged. "Not our business, but you should try to persuade her to stay in at night. Lots worse things can happen to her than being picked up by the cops."

He pursed his lips disapprovingly at Dr. McIntyre, then nodded at Laney. "Good luck, kid." He began to march down the stairs. "I've left her bike in the downstairs hall," he added over his shoulder.

The door closed behind him. Dr. McIntyre took

Laney's icy hands between his own. "I think," he said, "I'm going to make you a cup of cocoa."

It was so unlike what Laney expected that she gave a gulping sob. Her father pretended he hadn't heard. "You take a bath. Don't come out till you're warm. There's a robe behind the door."

"Don't you want to know—?"

"Later," he said.

She fled. When she was warm and smelling of soap and her face had gotten some of its color back, she found him in the kitchen. He was sitting blowing on his cocoa. And on the table in front of him, looking incongruous and small beside another steaming cup, was the little mask.

Blankly, she stared, first at it, then at him. "You went through my pack," she said dully.

"I'm sorry. I wanted to see if you had any extra clothes with you. But instead, I found this."

So now he knew. And she hadn't broken her promise to Mom. He had found the mask by himself.

"Sit down," he said, and pushed the other mug toward her.

She sat, eyeing him warily. How much could she tell him? How much would he even believe?

"Why did you have this little mask with you tonight?" he asked.

The heart of the issue. The very thing she couldn't answer. He was a scientist. He needed proof for everything. He wouldn't believe that Indian masks might control people. And he'd never believe that this small mask might stop another mask from possessing someone. From possessing—Mom.

"Are you going to answer my question?" Silence. "All right, we'll try again. Where did you get this mask? Who found it?"

"I did," Laney whispered. "It was in the bog. The same place I found the comb I showed you."

His eyes sharpened. "In *our* bog? You found an Iroquois false face mask in our bog?" She nodded. "But Laney, this whole territory belonged to Neutral Indians! No one's ever found—"

"I know. You told me the other day."

"Do you realize how important this is?" His eyes snapped with excitement.

"I wanted to tell you, but—"

He frowned. Then, very carefully, he examined the little mask again. "I see," he said. "Yes, I see." He looked at her. "This mask has been preserved. Did your mother do it?"

She took a big gulp of cocoa, her eyes dropping.

"Then she did." Her father's voice went cold. "She was going to sell it, wasn't she? No provenance, no questions asked, just off to the highest bidder, and no one ever to know that Neutral Indians had false face societies."

"I—she—but Dad, there's more to it than—"

"Go to bed, Laney."

"But—"

He saw the trouble in her face. His green eyes grew gentler. "I mean it. You're dead tired, and there's still school tomorrow. You can sleep in my bed. I'm finished with it for tonight."

"Can I—can I have the mask back? It *is* mine, Dad."

He looked right through her. His voice was remote. "No."

She stared at him desperately. But there was no wavering in him. He would keep it. He would confront her mother with it. Things had been bad enough. But now . . . She put her head in her hands.

"Go to bed," Dad said.

There was nothing to be done. She went.

LANEY AWOKE IN A POOL OF SUNLIGHT. FOR A MOMENT she lay still, frowning at the plaid blanket on the bed, the coffee-cream walls, the little antique chest across the room. The only thing that looked familiar was the bedside clock, a twin for her own. Her eyes widened. This was Dad's bedroom.

It was almost eleven. "Dad?" she called. She got out of bed, still wearing her father's robe. "Dad, are you there?"

The kitchen was tidy. There was no sign of the mask. On the table there was a note for her in her father's handwriting, and beside it, a second folded sheet. Laney sat down to read them.

Laney, the note said, *I've got an early lecture to give today, but I've written a note for the school to explain your lateness. About the small mask—your mother needn't find out how it came to me. But once and for all I intend to stop her from selling things like this. You're bound to feel caught in the crossfire, but it really has nothing to do with you. It's something between your mother and me, and it's been building for a long time. Don't blame yourself. Love, Dad.*

Nothing to do with her. Laney shook her head in disbelief. Did Dad really think that? And that business about Mom not having to know how he'd gotten the mask. How could he have gotten it, if not from Laney? Mom would be sure Laney had broken her promise and given it to him, and there was no way to tell her the truth without explaining the real reason why the mask had been in Laney's pack last night. And that was one thing Laney could never do.

And so Mom would think Laney didn't care enough about her to keep her out of a law court. She'd say she was as disloyal and moralistic as her father. Things between Laney and Alicia McIntyre would be changed forever.

If they weren't already, Laney thought wretchedly.

On a feverish impulse she picked up the phone to dial her father's office. He'd never let her give the little mask back to Mom, but maybe if she could convince him that Mom would be sure to blame her, he might just donate it to a museum and let Mom think she'd been burglarized. But the other end rang unanswered. Laney hung up, feeling desolate. Then she remembered the coldness of her father's voice when he'd first learned that Mrs. McIntyre was trying to sell the little mask. And she remembered how all through her parents' marriage Dad had never once given in to Mom; how he'd seemed to get *purposely* more absentminded, or more clumsy, or more of whatever else it was that bugged her, whenever she had nagged him about it. "You do it to spite me!" Mom had accused him, over and over again; and once, only once, he had yelled back, "I do it to keep my own soul!"

No, Dad had made up his mind, and he wouldn't change it. He was definitely going to confront Mom with the mask. Nothing that Laney could say or do would make one bit of difference.

And when he did, what would the large mask do? Would it—interfere?

It wouldn't. It would be glad that someone was going to take the small mask far away from it. It wouldn't do anything. Not unless Mom got really angry. . . .

But did Mom control it, really? Or did it control her? Or was it nothing but a dumb piece of wood, after all?

Laney rubbed her head, and rubbed it, but no answers came. All she knew for sure was that her parents were heading for their biggest fight ever, and that she was going to be caught in the middle. And today was October 31, too, Halloween, the day of masks. She wished she could laugh, but there was no humor inside her.

She got to school near the end of her lunch period. She wasn't hungry, but it was too cold and windy to sit outside, so she went into the lunchroom. She sat by herself, staring at a book she didn't even see. It was a surprise when Rosemary came up to her.

"You left the house pretty early this morning," her

sister said, her voice that half-accusing, half-placatory one she used when she wanted a favor. "I went to wake you at eight, but you were already gone."

"You don't usually get me up these days," Laney said.

"Well, I didn't want you to be late for school again."

"What *did* you want, then?"

The five-minute warning bell rang. Rosemary shifted from one foot to the other. "Listen, Laney, the kids're getting together after school tonight. A Halloween party."

"So?"

Rosemary's lips thinned, but she didn't walk off. Clearly she needed a favor. "Well, uh, listen," she said, "it'll probably last till ten. Will you tell Mom I'm at Lynn's?"

"But you're really going to Joe Winthrop's, aren't you?" Laney said it carelessly. Joe Winthrop was a kid in her sister's class. He didn't have a father, and every other month his mother worked till ten. His house was the site of a lot of parties. Mom didn't like Rosemary to go there.

"Hey, Sherlock Holmes," Rosemary said defiantly, "you're not doing me that big a favor. I can always phone Mom and tell her myself."

"Good idea." Laney gathered up her things, looking around the lunchroom. But there was no sign of Tom. He didn't know the police had stopped her last night.

He didn't even know that Dad now had the little mask.

"What's with you?" her sister said, genuinely puzzled. "You never acted like this before. You always—"

"See you," Laney said.

She was gone before her sister could react. Rosemary stared after her. Expressions flitted over her face, frustration, uncertainty, a kind of unwilling respect. Finally she walked off. For once, she hadn't found a single clever thing to say.

After school Laney took the bus downtown, going to the library and doing her math homework there. The calculator was an old friend by this time. She did things with it so automatically that sometimes she wasn't sure she'd used it at all. Math didn't scare her anymore, she realized, putting away her books. Now if only there were calculators for other kinds of problems . . .

Blankly she stared at the polished table, willing herself not to look up at the big library clock. But she couldn't stop herself. Quarter to five. Supper to make, and Mom's train coming in at seven. Ordinary life. She got to her feet. There was no point in putting it off any longer. Sooner or later she had to go home.

It was almost dark when the bus deposited her at the stop on Riverside Drive. The wind had blown itself out, but the cold it had brought remained. Laney could see her breath. The bus departed in a cloud of diesel fumes. She started walking, her shoulders hunched under the solid gray sky. In the west, where the last bit of sun ought to have been, the clouds were purplish and full of storm.

Across the street, on the track that led from the meadow, she saw the surveying van again, turn-signal blinking impatiently. The men in it were blanks behind the brilliance of their headlights. As she watched, the van seemed to fade away, and all that was left were those three lights, two steady, one blinking, like the eyes of something alien. The meadow dimmed into dusk behind it, and nothing could be seen of the trees at the edge of the bog.

Lost. The word whispered in her mind. Lost bog, lost tribe, lost knowledge, lost hopes. The long, slow process of dying that had begun the day she had dug up that mask. Everything had started then, the increased awkwardness with Mom, this new trouble between Mom and Dad, all that mess with the large mask, the fact that now no one would be able to prove Neutral Indians had had False Face Societies. And now the bog was going to be ruined, too, destroyed by the exhaust of bulldozers and trucks and by everything else that the development of the meadow would bring.

Had the bog been protected till now because the masks had been there, a center of Indian magic keeping itself safe despite the twentieth-century city that surrounded it? It was a new thought. Dispiritedly Laney considered it. A quarter of a million people living and working a stone's throw away, and nothing had happened to that bog; and before that, no farmers had drained it for the plough, and no nineteenth-century board of health had decided it was a source of disease and ought to be eradicated. No, everything had been fine with the bog until she had taken the little mask from it.

Slowly she began walking again. It was very cold. Her hands, her feet, were numb. She felt as if she had a lump of ice in her chest. At her front sidewalk, she stopped. There was someone sitting on the porch. It was Tom.

"I've been waiting for you," he said, from all that distance away. He frowned then, peering through the gloom at her. "You look awful. Are you okay?"

She moved toward him. The ice melted a little. "You weren't at school today."

He shrugged. "I was sleeping. You wouldn't think anybody could, after last night. You sure you're all right?"

"Can you—stay for a while?"

"Yeah, sure. If you want me to."

She was closer now, close enough for a whisper to be heard. Her lips moved. "Tom, Dad has the small mask. He's going to show it to Mom."

His eyes widened. "What happened? How did he—?"

She sat down beside him on the cold concrete steps and told him everything. "Maybe you should come home with me for a while," Tom said, when he'd heard it all.

"It'd just postpone things," Laney said. Her voice was so desolate he took her hand. The streetlights were on. Outside, the whole world was dark.

"I'll stay till after your mom comes home," Tom said. And then, "Don't worry, Laney. We'll think of something."

But he knew—they both knew—they wouldn't.

Six-thirty. The doorbell rang. Laney opened the door. A tiny witch waited, half drowned in her hat, her cardboard mask too large for her face. "Tickateet," she whispered behind it, while a man hovered protectively beside her.

For a moment Laney could only stare. Then she remembered. Trick or treat. Halloween. Candy. "Just a minute," she said, trying to think. Licorice, she thought, in the kitchen.

They came quickly then, dozens of them. Hambone almost went crazy with barking. Laney finally shut him in the basement. Between rings of the doorbell she looked at the clock. Seven o'clock. Seven-thirty. "When does your mother's train get in?" Tom asked.

"It should be here already," she said. Neither of them spoke again.

Eight o'clock. The doorbell was ringing less frequently now. And when it did, they were older kids, as old as Laney, some of them. Horrible masks leered at her from the shadows, laughing when she jumped. She was running out of licorice. They wouldn't like it if she had to give apples.

Eight-thirty-five. The doorbell hadn't rung for almost fifteen minutes. Tom was pacing restlessly. Hambone was whining behind the basement door. Laney was counting licorice treats. *Ring!* She opened the door.

And standing there, silent under the porch light, was the mask from the bog.

Laney shrieked, then tried to slam the door against the thing outside. But it had legs and arms and was stronger than she was. "Help, Tom, help!" He dashed from the living room, but it was too late. The mask was already inside.

Laney fell back. Tom stood beside her. They were both very pale. A familiar voice came from behind the mask. "Two stags at bay," it said and laughed.

Mrs. McIntyre stripped off the mask. She was rather flushed, and her eyes were brilliant. She held the mask casually by a new cord strung at the back, the *face* turned downward, out of view. Her voice, when she spoke, was amused. "I hardly expected to get a reaction like that. After all, it is Halloween."

"That's no Halloween mask," Tom said loudly, "and you know it."

Mrs. McIntyre looked him slowly up and down. It was a labeling look, entirely insolent. Tom knew exactly what she was thinking. She turned to Laney. "Who is this—boy?" she asked. "And where is your sister?"

Laney's eyes were fixed on the mask, swinging so casually from her mother's hand. Hatred. She could feel it. It was like sinking in quicksand, an oozing suffocation. Why did it hate her so? She didn't hear her mother. She scarcely saw her. Her face had the bluish tinge of someone in deep shock.

"I asked you a question, Laney," Mrs. McIntyre said.

Somehow Laney took her eyes from the mask, turning them like green lamps on her mother's face. "What did you say?" she whispered.

Instinctively Tom put his body between them. The woman stared at him so haughtily that his hands clenched into fists. "I'm Tom Walsh," he answered for Laney. His chin was high, his cheekbones jutting. "And Laney's sister is at a party."

The blue eyes glittered at him. "What are you doing in my house?"

"It's Laney's house, too, isn't it?" Tom challenged her. "Can't she ask her friends to come in?"

"My daughters do not have boys in unless somebody else is home. Laney knows that. You'd better go."

My daughters. My house. My mask, too, the way she was handling it. Suddenly Tom hated her. "I won't go," he said. "Not until Laney tells me to."

Laney spoke up then. There was a little more color in her face, but she kept her eyes averted from the mask. "Mom, please, I did ask Tom to stay. I—"

"When you knew Rosemary would be out?" Her mother's lips thinned. "You and I have some serious talking to do, Laney." The hand holding the mask swung a little harder. "And I mean alone."

Alone, Tom thought. All by herself with her mother and the mask. No one there to distract it from Laney, no little mask to protect her, nothing to stand between Laney and the hatred. Mrs. McIntyre's eyes were like twin ice cubes. Tom looked sideways into them, and his stomach gave a lurch. He couldn't leave Laney here with her! But how could he prevent it? Then, suddenly, he knew.

"Mrs. McIntyre. Mrs. McIntyre!" Slowly she turned her eyes his way. They had a blind look that terrified him. "That's a nice mask you've got there," he said. His voice was loud, and much too high. He got it under control. "The Ontario Ministry of Culture would be really impressed. Maybe I should call them, tell them to have a look?"

The hand swinging the mask stilled. For a brief moment nobody moved. Fury and tension sang in the air, a high-pitched humming like electricity. And then the doorbell rang.

Saved by the bell, Tom thought wildly.

The blindness in Mrs. McIntyre's eyes faded. She

frowned, but not at Tom. Her expression cleared. She was just inside the door, but instead of answering the bell she walked to the end of the foyer, passing Laney without touching her. "You get it, Laney," she said very calmly.

Laney shook her head as if to clear it. Then she went to the door. She opened it, automatically reaching for the bowl of Halloween treats. Abruptly her hand stilled. She gave a little sighing gulp. A man's voice sounded from the porch outside.

"Hello, Laney. Is your mother home?"

"Yes," Laney said, throwing a hunted look over her shoulder. "Yes, Dad, she is."

HE WAS RATHER SMALL FOR A MAN, AND THIN, WITH A lined, grave face. His hair and eyes were Laney's color exactly. His left hand gripped a paper bag, but the other hung loose, the fingers rather short, the palms wide and capable. Tom looked at those hands and recognized them: Laney's hands, bigger and browner, but otherwise identical. Dr. McIntyre was following Laney in. He held himself straighter than Laney, but there was something about the way he moved, a tension, a self-contained neatness, that was very much like her. If it were not for the stubborn set to the man's shoulders and the jut to his chin, Tom might have thought he was seeing two generations of twins.

"Hello, Alicia," Dr. McIntyre said.

"Ian," she acknowledged coolly. The hand holding the mask was behind her back against the wall.

Laney stopped at Tom's side. "Dad, this is Tom Walsh," she said, struggling for normalcy. "He's a friend of mine."

"How do you do, Tom?" Dr. McIntyre said, offering his hand.

"Fine, thanks," Tom said. He cast a quick look toward Mrs. McIntyre, then back to the bag in Dr. McIntyre's hand. The miniature mask was in it, he was sure. The small mask, in the same room as the full-sized mask that hated it. Tom didn't dare look at Laney.

"—don't often get a chance to meet Laney's friends," Dr. McIntyre was saying. "Are you two in the same class?"

Mrs. McIntyre's voice broke in. "Let's not pretend this is a social call, Ian. What are you doing here?"

He walked toward her, his measured steps taking him to within an arm's length of her. She didn't move. Holding that illegal mask, knowing what her former husband would do if he found it, yet unflinching . . . Tom almost admired her in that moment.

"I have something in here I want to talk to you about," Dr. McIntyre told her, holding up the paper bag. "Shall we go into your workroom?"

Alicia's tongue flicked her bottom lip. "I don't think that'll be necessary," she said evenly. "Nothing you have to say ever takes more than a few minutes. Get it over with, and then get out."

Hatred filled the room, bog-thick and smothering. Laney struggled against it, against the nightmare images swimming dizzily past her vision. *Turtles, their tails cut off, hanging till the last drop of red falls sticky into the pool beneath. Put in the cherry pits, stop up the openings, let only the rattling escape.* Laney leaned against the wall. Her heart was a drum, thudding, thudding. Her mind was hazy as longhouse smoke. *Rattle. Rattle.* Summon the people, summon the god, summon the hatred, let it all come to pass. Nothing could stop it anyway; nothing could change what was to be. Events to be played out, events she had started. And the Round Dance to come and Death on the longhouse floor.

Tom saw her face. Alarmed, he headed toward her. But Dr. McIntyre spoke then, and the threat in his voice was so striking it stopped him in his tracks. "What I have to say may take longer than usual, Alicia. Unless, that is, you decide to do all your answering to a judge."

Mrs. McIntyre's eyes narrowed. "What *are* you talking about?"

"I'm talking about Indian artifacts. About selling them. Masks, in particular." Without taking his eyes off her, he unrolled the paper bag and reached inside. "This mask." And he held it up.

Outside the longhouse, a little girl is trembling. When you are bad, her mother has said, the false faces will get you.

Briefly, very briefly, Mrs. McIntyre's eyes slid to Laney and back again. "Where did you get that?" she asked softly.

"Maybe Laney and I should—" Tom began.

Mrs. McIntyre glared at him. He shut up.

"Someone broke into the house here last night," Ian McIntyre said. "Today this was made available to me."

"How did you know it came from here?" Alicia said skeptically.

"I—found out."

"Obviously," she said, again with that serpentine look at Laney.

Dr. McIntyre shoved out his chin even farther. "The point is," he said, "you were intending to sell this, and I won't have it."

Mrs. McIntyre laughed. "The point is, how are you going to prove it?"

"I'll prove it if I have to," Ian said. "I'm not letting you get away with this kind of thing any more."

"I'm a dealer. I sell old things. It's my job."

"Well, it's *my* job to stop you from selling our history out from under us!"

"Your job? Your job is to molder away in the classroom! Who promoted you to public defender?"

Through his teeth, Dr. McIntyre said, "This mask is one of a kind. It's the only proof we've got that a Neutral tribe near our bog had False Face Societies—"

"So Laney did give it to you."

He stared at her.

"Oh come on," she said impatiently, "only Laney could have told you it was found in our bog. For God's sake, Ian, do you think I'm a fool?"

"You're many things, but you're not that."

"Mom, I didn't give it to him. Please, Mom, I—"

"You're so much like him, Laney, it makes me sick. You've always been like him. I looked at you in your cradle, and there he was."

"That's not—I try all the time to—Mom!"

Icily Alicia said, "You made me a promise, and you broke it."

"She didn't," Dr. McIntyre said. "I found the mask in her pack when she came over to my house last night. She never intended me to have it. But even if she had—"

"Why did she come to you, then?"

"—even if she had, she wouldn't be the first person to break a promise. I seem to remember you made *me* a promise once. In a church."

"For God's sake, Ian, will you get off that pulpit?" Her shoulders jerked as she turned to Laney, and briefly Tom glimpsed the large mask she was holding behind her back. He wondered if Dr. McIntyre could see it, too. "What were you up to, Laney? Why did you take that small mask with you? You little fool, what were you trying to do?"

Laney was pressed against the other wall. She wasn't crying, but there was a look on her face that made Tom almost wish she was.

"Leave her alone," Dr. McIntyre said. "You always attack someone when you're in the wrong. And this time you've outdone yourself. How could you even consider selling this mask? I give you plenty of money, and the store is doing well. You can't need cash that badly. And God knows, you've studied enough anthropology to realize what harm you were doing. If I hadn't stopped you, you would have—"

"The honorable scientist with no vested interest," she jeered. "I suppose you're not going to write up finding the small mask? Nothing in it for you? Oh, never. Just a report of an important finding in an important journal, with Dr. Ian McIntyre as the first author."

"All important new information has to be reported." Woodenly.

"And this is important, isn't it? You write this up, and you'll be lording it over your colleagues for the rest of your academic life. That's what this is really about, isn't it? Money in the bank, Ian; it's the same for both of us!"

Expressions chased each other over Dr. McIntyre's face. Finally he found his voice. "One of your most disconcerting features, Alicia, is that you're always just a little bit right." He squared his shoulders. "What are you hiding behind your back?"

"Nothing." It came too quickly.

"Show me." Laney's father's free hand went out, stopping a hairbreadth from her elbow. His other hand still held the small mask. Tom looked at Laney, willing her to get away, to come home with him and let the two adults fight it out. But her eyes were deep pools and lost to him, and he couldn't leave without her.

Mrs. McIntyre recoiled as much as she could with the wall behind her. "This isn't your house, Ian. I want you to leave."

"Is it something else you're selling illegally? It is, isn't it?" He was crowding her again.

"Do I have to call the police?"

"Good idea. We'll let them find out what you're up to."

Tension hummed between them like the sound of old lamps burning their last, wires sizzling, fires threatening. Tom heard it, and under the tension something else, the suck and plop of evil things rising from a swamp. The masks, loathing one another, yet made to be together; made to hide the face beneath, yet revealing it, too.

"Let me see!" Ian McIntyre grunted, his hand closing tight on Alicia's elbow.

"I'm warning you!"

"Let me see!"

And he pulled on her arm, twisting it forward, hurting. "I warned you," she shouted. "I did warn you, Ian!" And then something happened, something the others could only feel.

Tom shuddered. When his eyes cleared, he could see sweat on Dr. McIntyre's forehead. The older man was so white little freckles stood out. He gave a queer sort of groan, but kept on pulling on Mrs. McIntyre's arm. The little mask was almost touching her. Slowly, and more slowly, the hand behind Mrs. McIntyre's back was coming forward. At last the large mask was visible.

Dr. McIntyre dropped her arm. His free hand went to his face. Laney cried out, a single sharp cry. In the basement Hambone began to howl. And then mask faced mask, and the world went dark.

Somewhere, someone was vomiting. Laney heard it through the darkness that sucked at her. Hatred. Hatred. Don't you love me, then? I'm a part of you; don't you love me?

"Laney!" Tom shook at her arm. "Laney, you've got to help him. Laney!"

She blinked. It was a voice she knew. But she couldn't see. She was blind, lost in a world without color. "Help him?" Help someone else, when it was all she could do to survive the hatred herself?

"Your father! He's vomiting blood. Laney, she's killing him!"

Black over red, the halved masks severed. Death over life. Inevitable.

But Dad, Daddy, dying?

"Try. Laney, you've got to!"

She tried. She did what she could. She opened her mind to the power of the little mask, willing it to heal her father, but there was a barrier there. The small mask would not let her be weakened, would not let the other mask destroy her. Outside her sight, the sound of vomiting was weaker. A man's breath was rattling in his chest. Turtle-rattling, a shell with stones. The drip-drip-drip of blood being silenced forever.

There was a way, and Laney knew it. She could fight the large mask with the small. Power against power, black against black: It was a choice; it was open to her. Briefly her eyes cleared, and she saw the mask on her mother's face. Mom had made her choice, but still Laney could not make her own.

She turned away then, looking for her father. He was unclear, a black outline only, surrounded by red. But she saw clearly the small mask clutched in his hand. It was useless to him. It couldn't protect *him* from the large mask. It could protect only Laney, its rightful owner.

Unless she gave it to him. Unless she let it go.

But if she did that, the other mask would be free to destroy her. And it was trying to do that. It was trying even now. It hated her. It hated Laney as if she were the same person as her father.

Mom, oh, Mom.

Nothing mattered. Nothing could help her. The power of the small mask was being wasted. "Go," she said to it. The little mask was already in her father's hand. Now she made it belong there. It went like a great bird, its spirit lifting him and raising him to safety, even as Laney fell.

"Laney!" Tom jumped to her side, clutching her.

Her face was blank, ashen, eyes facing the unknown, welcoming it. He had seen that kind of face on someone before. He knew what he was looking at.

In a fury, half-sobbing, he turned to the woman wearing the mask. "Stop it! *Stop!* It's not Laney's fault she looks like him!"

The great blind eyes turned his way, but he had gone beyond fear. He was back on the Reserve where people looked at him and saw a white; he was in London where kids said "How" to him instead of "Hello"; he was in his own house looking at his mother and seeing only the color of her skin.

"There's somebody *in* there behind those looks!" Tom cried, to Mrs. McIntyre, to all of them, to himself. "You don't know who she is; you never even tried to find out. You just looked and decided, and the real person never had a chance! And she loves you; she tries and tries; *he* never tried, but *she* does. Just to please you, she tries to be what you want. And you—we—"

He was weeping, and he didn't care, standing rigid over Laney with the blinding tears coursing down his face. Mom, I'm sorry, oh, Mom, Mom. And Laney, and Dr. McIntyre, and Dad, and Tom himself. Grief, so much grief. His harsh sobs were the only sound in all that pain-filled room. Tears, not red and not black, not white and not Indian. Just tears, from some-one who was a person, nothing else.

The mask of Gaguwara was approaching him, but

Tom didn't see. Lost in grief, he stood, while the undrilled wooden eyes came closer and closer. Slowly, Mrs. McIntyre's hand went out, and her white finger touched Tom's wet cheek. Then, with the tears still on it, that finger hooked the chin of the mask, lifted it up, and shoved it backward until it fell to the floor.

A minute passed. Tom scrubbed his eyes, but otherwise he didn't move. Uncertainly he watched Mrs. McIntyre bending over Laney, raising her by the elbow, feeling her forehead. When Laney blinked up at her, she stepped back. Dr. McIntyre got to his feet. He seemed quite well, though his freckles still stood out. There was no blood in the vomit on the carpet.

But there had been blood, Tom thought wonderingly. Hadn't he seen it, red in the darkness, a life pouring out into the night?

The little mask was securely in the older man's hand. He looked at it, then bent down, reaching for the larger one. "Be careful," Tom got out. "It's still—she still owns it."

"No," Mrs. McIntyre said. Her voice was thick and hoarse. She was wiping her fingers against her skirt. "I don't want it. You take it, Ian." She turned away, running shaking fingers through her hair. "You will anyway," she added, in her more usual voice.

Laney's father let his hand close on the mask on the floor. Tom held his breath. Nothing happened.

He sagged with relief. So it was finished, he told himself. The same person now owned both masks. The war was under control.

Dr. McIntyre sat down tiredly in a chair and began rather absently to braid the hair of the two masks together. He was looking doubtfully at Laney. "I don't remember very much after Alicia—after that large mask—" He broke off. "You're all right, aren't you?"

Laney nodded. She was still very pale, but the look that had terrified Tom was gone. Her eyes were deep and green and full of pain, twin mirrors for her father's. Neither of them looked at Alicia.

"It was you who was sick, Ian, not Laney," Mrs. McIntyre said in a brittle voice.

"Why did you give me this mask, Alicia?"

She shrugged. "Now that you know it exists, you'll never let me sell it." So already the denial was beginning, Tom thought. By next week she would have convinced herself that selling it was all she'd ever wanted to do.

"I don't want it," Dr. McIntyre retorted. "I don't want either of them." He held the two masks out to Tom. "They're your heritage. You'll know the best thing to do with them."

Tom frowned incredulously. "You want me to be their rightful owner? But these masks could make you famous."

"Money in my bank, you mean? Look, I didn't discover the masks. Why should I cash in on them?"

"Ian, Ian, Ian," Mrs. McIntyre said lightly, searching her purse for a lipstick, "is there nothing you won't do to avoid fame and fortune?" But her lightness was forced, and the hand that was gripping the purse was shaking.

Dr. McIntyre was still holding out the masks. Tom felt sadness sweep over him. The white people didn't want the masks; the Society of Faces didn't want them. But someone had to take charge of them. His hands went out and gathered them to him. He wouldn't keep them. No one could own those two masks, not without the risk of being owned by them, too. Dr. McIntyre was right. The only safety from the masks lay in giving them up.

"Aren't you even going to tell people that the Neutrals had False Face Societies?" Laney asked her father.

"Telling's no good without proof." He shrugged. "I will prove it, though, someday. Now that I know it's possible, nothing's going to stop me." He gave her a tiny smile. "It's kind of like that slide rule," he added.

She nodded, not smiling, but clearly understanding. Then she got to her feet and went to stand beside him. As Tom looked at them, his sadness almost turned to jealousy. They were so much alike! Their shared appearance was a bond, rooting them so that they never had to feel alone. Then he saw Laney's dark green eyes regarding him. Size, shape, color, all were identical to her father's, but they were Laney's eyes, and they were looking at him in a way no person had ever done before.

One day, he thought, he would paint her like this. And when the painting was right, when it was perfect, he would send it to that new national gallery, and then everybody would see what he saw in her. White, Indian, half-breed, what did it matter? Nobody was free, and nobody was safe. Everybody had to choose what to let himself be.

"It's going to be all right," he told her. He fumbled for the doorknob, the masks in one hand. The bog was where they had come from, where they belonged. He would give them back to it, to a place, rather than a person. He would choose a spot far away from the body that had once owned them, a spot with no landmarks to remind him where. And after he sank them deep, deep in the muck, in a place where they could never be recovered, he would go away and try to forget even the feel of them in his hand.

The door closed behind him. Now there were only the three of them. An uncomfortable silence fell. Mrs. McIntyre made a pretense of examining the mess on the carpet. "You must have eaten something really rotten, Ian," she said. "I think I'd better call the doctor." She walked quickly out, and they could hear her dialing.

Laney looked at her father. "I've tried so hard," she whispered. "I've done everything I could to be what she wanted."

"And I didn't try enough," he said.

"At least you stayed your own person."

"I stayed the person I had decided to be. Was that so good? I don't know. And you, you were so busy trying not to be me, that was all you *could* be, in front of your mother."

She heard his hurt. "I'm sorry," she said miserably. "It wasn't because I didn't like you. It's just that—oh, Dad, I loved her so much."

Loved. Desolation swept her. It was something she had had forever, a mother she had loved. And now that love was gone, buried in the wooden gaze of an Iroquois mask.

"It can be—freeing," Dad said tentatively, "not to have to care too much. But you might be surprised, Laney. You might come to love her again."

"When she hates me?"

"It's me she hates, not you. Tom knew the difference. So did she, in the end. And she took off that mask, Laney; it had almost taken her over, but she fought it, and she won. God knows how, but she did."

He paused. His voice became deep, his words slow and careful. "She doesn't know you; that's the thing. *You* don't know you. Maybe, when you've both figured out who you are, she'll like you; maybe she won't. But it'll be because of what you are, not because of an idea of you she has. There's one thing I can tell you for sure, Laney. Your mother's going to pretend that nothing terrible happened here today, but deep in her heart, she knows it has. She'll never forget, her whole life long, that she hated someone almost enough to kill."

And I hated Rosemary almost enough to kill, too, Laney thought, and I'll never forget it, either. It was a bond they had, she and Mom, a starting point.

The black and the red, the hating and the loving, the two savage, eternal halves struggling beneath civilized appearances. False faces everywhere, Laney thought. Masks on masks on masks.

But there were still the Toms, and there were still the Dads. She reached for her father, and he was there, arms tight, shutting everything else away.

The door opened, and Rosemary came in. "I just saw Injun Joe coming out our front—" She broke off. "Oh, yucch, somebody's been sick all over the carpet!"

Neither Laney nor her father heard. Hambone, in the basement, was making a noise remarkably like yodeling. Mrs. McIntyre was speaking to the doctor on the phone. "Can I send him home, or should I—? No, he's stopped vomiting. All right. Thanks." She hung up.

And catching a glimpse of Rosemary in the hall, she called out, "Get a bucket and some rags, will you, Rosemary? I could use some help. And no one gave you permission to go to a party, by the way."

But Rosemary, conveniently deaf, had already disappeared.

EPILOGUE

THE THREATENING STORM HAD COME TO NOTHING. THE banks of clouds had disappeared into the night. Overhead the sky stretched to infinity, the deep blackness of space interrupted by the pinprick comfort of stars. Under it the bog breathed its cold November breath, a silvery fog the moonlight made magic.

Where the ospreys hunted by day a lone muskrat stirred. The human had gone, and the thing he had dropped, weighted with a stone, had long since ceased to cause even a bubble in the smooth surface of mud. But the muskrat remained active in its haystack house. It wasn't disturbed, merely alive and aware of it. Safe.

Across the city, a man was sitting reading at his desk. He had been asleep, but a dream had awakened him. Now he was working, trying to get the taste of the dream out of his mind. He was reading a new letter from the persistent Dr. McIntyre. As usual it was about the bog. *Neutral Indians* . . . he read. . . . *potential for archaeological value. Ecological damage incalculable* . . .

He read on and on. Outside, the moon was a globe,

cold and dominating and demanding. The man put down his papers and went to his window. Night was a giant place. There seemed room for anything in it.

Except, perhaps, Man.

He would have no end of trouble over that bog, anyway. And how much was money really worth, in the end?

"What the hell," the man said suddenly.

He went back to his desk. He scrawled something on a piece of paper. *Sell meadow and bog to the city for permanent parkland.* He smiled. *Price: $1.00.*

"And if that doesn't get me some good publicity," he said aloud, "nothing will."

He went back to bed and dreamed of a key to the city.

AUTHOR'S NOTE

I got the idea for False Face after visiting the Museum of Indian Archaeology in London, Ontario. One of the artifacts in this fascinating museum is a modern Iroquois false face mask, and beside it is an empty space where another face mask has indeed been removed because of its "sensitive nature." I would like to thank the museum's Catherine Comrie and Debra Bodner, who gave me useful advice and helped in my research.

The Iroquois peoples were already in Canada in 1535 when Jacques Cartier, the French explorer, reached North America, but they were later driven south by the Algonquins to what is now known as North Carolina. There they formed a confederacy for their own protection. They called themselves the Five Nations and comprised the tribes of Mohawks, Oneidas, Onondagas, Cayugas, and Senecas. Later the Tuscaroras joined them, and the union became the Six Nations. (It was the French who called them the Iroquois.) In 1712 they were driven out of North Carolina and settled in New York State. In the Revolutionary War, Joseph Brant led the Mohawks and Cayugas into Canada, where the Canadian government gave them several reservations, one of which is the Six Nations Reserve on the Grand River near Brantford, Ontario.

Although many people on this Reserve are now Christians, a fair number still practice the longhouse religion. Once, the Iroquois people actually lived in longhouses, but now the longhouses are merely ceremonial centers. The longhouse religion is centered on the teachings of the Iroquois prophet Handsome Lake. In several of its sacred rituals masks take a vital part, worn to invoke the power of the supernatural beings whose faces the masks represent. The lesser masks are made of corn husks, but the more powerful ones are of wood. The most important of all is the false face I wrote about in this book, the face of the "Great Doctor."

This godlike being has different names within the Six Nations. Gaguwara is one, Shagodyoweh another. He carries a huge staff and a giant rattle made from the shell of a snapping turtle filled with cherry pits. His face is red in the morning and black in the afternoon. According to legend, the Doctor's first conflict with the Creator resulted in his being hit in the face by a mountain, giving him his pain-filled look. But the Creator realized his power after this conflict and so charged him with the task of driving disease from the earth. The False Face agreed to give the Indians the power to cure by the blowing of hot ashes onto a sick person, as long as they carved masks in his image and made him offerings of respect—maize and tobacco. His power could be dangerous, however, and so sometimes miniature masks were carved as amulets of protection.

Almost without exception each full-sized mask is carved by the individual who will wear it. He goes alone into the forest and finds a living tree, usually basswood. After propitiating the spirits by offering prayers and burning tobacco, he carves the mask into the tree. Only after the mask is finished is it cut out of the tree. Eyeholes are then drilled (except for certain very old, blind masks), and metal is often used to highlight the holes. Masks have varying kinds of noses and mouths but are almost always grimacing with pain. Some masks, like the ones in this book, are painted half red and half black, to indicate the changing and dual face of the god they represent.

The spirit of the Great Doctor is summoned to longhouse ceremonies as well as to individual sickbeds by the Society of Faces. This Society comprises people who have had a dream of the masks or who have themselves been cured by a False Face ceremony. They put on their masks and make a great racket with horns and rattles to summon everyone to the ceremony. They dance and chant and blow hot ashes on the sick person, and then everyone (including the sick person) is made to dance the Round Dance. People who refuse are forced. Some people go into trances or have "fits" during these ceremonies. Others either catch or are cured of the False Face sickness, usually a disease of the mouth or head (such as emotional or mental disorders, headaches, facial growths), but sometimes of the respiratory tract.

We know that these masks are a very old tradition, because the French explorers recorded their use early in the sixteenth century. A very few masks remain from the early centuries, but most of these were never buried in the earth. Corn husks and wood rot in ordinary earth. But a true bog has the right chemical ingredients and conditions to preserve organic material. Some very ancient Iroquois false faces were recently found in a bog near Toronto. I am very grateful to the Archaeological Field Unit of the Ministry of Citizenship and Culture of Ontario for giving me this information and so patiently answering my many questions.

The bog I used in my book is similar to a real bog in London, Ontario. However, the developer I refer to is not a real person. He is my invention only.

In this book I have attempted, with only a little leeway, to be accurate about Iroquois songs and False Face rituals. For the Iroquois songs I used in the book, my main reference was a book by Gertrude Prokosch Kurath, Dance and Song Rituals of Six Nations Reserve, Ontario *(National Museum of Canada, Bulletin 220, 1968). Another extremely interesting source is W. N. Fenton's* Masked Medicine Societies of the Iroquois *(the Smithsonian Institution, 1940).*

I am extremely grateful to the Canada Council for the Project Grant that enabled me to work on this book. In addition I appreciated very much the readings and suggestions of my friends Joan Finegan and Barbara Novak. I also want to acknowledge Barbara's kindness in allowing me to quote the last stanza of her poem, Pale Answers, *at the beginning of the book.*

Last, I want to thank my husband, Albert Katz, for all his time-giving help as well as for his suggestions on this book and his support for my writing in general. Without him, this book, and all the others, would not have been possible.